The
INITIATE
IN THE DARK CYCLE

MW00437700

The INITIATE
IN THE DARK CYCLE

Cyril Scott

SAMUEL WEISER, INC.

York Beach, Maine

This edition published in 1991 by
Samuel Weiser, Inc.
Box 612
York Beach, ME 03910

First published in 1932 by Routledge & Kegan Paul, Ltd.
First paperback edition, 1977
Fifth printing, 1992

Copyright © 1991 The estate of Cyril Scott
All rights reserved. No part of this publication may be repro-
duced or transmitted in any form or by any means, electronic or
mechanical, including photocopy, without permission in writing
from Samuel Weiser, Inc.

Library of Congress Cataloging-in-Publication Data

Scott, Cyril. 1879-1970.
    The initiate in the dark cycle : a sequel to "The initiate" and
to "The initiate in the new world" / by his pupil.
        p.   cm.
    Reprint. Originally published: London : Routledge &
Kegan Paul, 1932.
    1. Haig. Justin Moreward. 2. Spiritual life. 3. Occultists.
4. Gurus. I. Title.
  BF1408.2.H35S35   1991
  133'.092--dc20   90-23037
  [B]   CIP

ISBN 0-87728-362-1
BJ

Cover illustration is entitled "Time Travelers" copyright © 1988
Rob Schouten. Used by kind permssion of the artist.

Printed in the United States of America

The paper used in this publication meets the minimum requirements of the American National Standard for Permanence of
Paper for Printed Library Materials Z39.48-1984.

TO

THOSE WHO HAVE STOOD
THE TEST

CONTENTS

INTRODUCTION

At a time when mighty cosmic changes are taking place in the unseen worlds, and corresponding changes and upheavals on the physical plane, the Masters of Wisdom have done me the honour to suggest that I write this second sequel to *The Initiate*. Their object is to give out a little more knowledge and enlightenment to a sadly bewildered humanity, and more especially to those students of the Higher Occultism who for some time have been faced, and still are faced, with problems they feel quite unable to solve. The nature of those problems and the *modus operandi* employed by the Masters for transmitting the necessary knowledge will be revealed in the book itself. Their suggestion and its fulfilment, moreover, may incidentally serve the personal and much less important purpose of extricating me from a number of dilemmas in which as the result of my previous books I have become involved.

For I have been made the target for a host of letters, questions and demands with which, for the most part, I have but inadequately been able to cope. Some of the writers of these letters, which have come from all parts of the world, have requested me to induce my Guru to accept them as pupils; others have begged me to ask him to intervene in their troubles and difficulties or those of their friends; others again have demanded interviews with myself as a preliminary step to meeting him. With lavish expenditure of self-praise, some of them have enumerated the many and varied qualifications which they consider entitle them to become his pupils. Wives have written to me, asking how they should deal with unfaithful husbands, and husbands how they should deal with unfaithful wives. In short, what do I think the Initiate Justin Moreward Haig would advise in their particular case? I have even received threats to the effect that if I do not reveal how the Initiate performed his so-called " miracles," [1] I am to be considered lacking in a true sense of brotherhood, since no Lord of Compassion would ever keep

[1] See *The Initiate in the New World*, Chapter XVI.

knowledge to Himself, but would share it with others !

Though some of these correspondents profess their admiration for my books (for which, by the way, I take this opportunity to thank them), they yet put me questions which, to all intents and purposes, have been answered in the books themselves—a fact which implies either that they have not fully grasped their significance, or that they have done what certain people are apt to do in connection with the Bible—namely, accept those particular teachings which suit their convenience, and ignore the others.

Fortunately the more embarrassing types of communication only show one side of the picture. I have received many other letters declaring that their writers have been practically saved from conjugal shipwreck by the teachings of the Initiate. Others generously maintain that he has been instrumental in completely transforming their outlook on life ; others, again, that they have been helped by the books while in the throes of some material or emotional crisis.

In writing this introduction, however, so much of which has dealt with the subject of correspondence, I do not wish to discourage any reader who feels impelled to write to me regarding questions which have not been already touched upon in the books themselves. On the other hand, I do earnestly remind my readers for their own sakes that it is useless for them to write and ask me to effect a meeting with my Master, for they will see, if they have the patience to read this third book, *how* and *why* such a request cannot be granted. Furthermore they will realize, as they do not appear to have done from reading the introduction to my last book, that I am not in a position to satisfy those who have endeavoured, or who may still endeavour, to persuade me to discard all discretion and tell them outright who the Initiate is, and where he may be found. As, however, a rumour has been circulated to the effect that the real J. M. H. is Bishop Wedgewood, a dignitary of the Liberal Catholic Church, and I have received letters asking if this is correct, I will here quite unequivocally state that the rumour is false. It may have been possible to write the biography of an inebriate poet without even mentioning soda-water—for such a biography has actually appeared—but it would hardly be feasible to write a book about a bishop and never once mention the Church ! In any case, Gurus who live in the Western world— and this is an important point—cannot conduct their mundane affairs after the manner of some of the Indian Yogis or Saddhus, who seem prepared to deliver little homilies to anyone who wishes to listen, and do not seem averse from having books and pamphlets written about them, proclaiming their saintliness and exact whereabouts. In fact, despite their unworldliness, they would appear to have no objection to becoming public characters. But conditions in the East and conditions in the West are widely dissimilar. No Western Guru or Master whom I have ever heard of is a public character. It is one thing for the Mahatmas, who inaccessibly reside in the fastnesses of Tibet, to permit books to be written, describing Their environment, and quite another for European Masters to permit a similar disclosure. No book has been written indicating the actual whereabouts of, say, the English Masters, one of the reasons being that the publication of such a book would lead to disastrous attacks on

Their privacy, and thus interfere with the important work which They, in common with all other Adepts, are doing for Humanity.

And so let it here be clearly stated that the books I have written were never penned with the intention of " advertising " my Guru as an easily accessible Teacher *in the flesh* for all and sundry who feel themselves entitled to occult training, but for the more expansive purpose of testifying to the existence of those Great Ones, the Gurus, Adepts and Masters, who modestly term Themselves the Elder Brothers of Humanity. In the first place, there are those people who have never heard of the Adepts, and consequently do not believe in Them ; secondly, there are those who would like to believe in Their existence but find themselves unable to do so ; and thirdly, there are the most unfortunate of all—those who, having once believed, have come to be assailed by grievous doubts. Those of the first category need not detain us, but those of the second and third are perhaps in a position to be helped by the testimony of one who has definite knowledge in contradistinction to mere belief. For the knowledge of one person who has *seen* may at any rate inspire belief in the minds of those who have not seen, and in the world of occultism, belief can eventually lead to knowledge. Already to believe in the Masters of Wisdom and to subscribe to Their teachings, is to establish a telepathic link with Them ; or, as we would say in these days of wireless, is to " tune in," as it were, to Their vibrations.

But apart from this, at various periods in the world's history the Masters are ready with Their advice and Their Teachings, to adjust the balance of changing morals, customs and beliefs. That my Guru added his contribution to the output of these Teachings I have endeavoured to show, however inadequately, in these impressions which he has permitted me to write.

Let us, however, have no misunderstandings at the outset. I who have chosen to call myself Charles Broadbent am neither a spiritual nor a literary " big-bug," as doubtless critical and observant persons have gathered from my previous books. My life has not been that of a saint, and my literary powers leave so much to be desired that I feel the whole task should have been allotted to a biographer or novelist of repute instead of

to me.   Yet strange to say, no such novelist
has been forthcoming.   As for saints, they
may with difficulty be able to write about
mystical states of consciousness, but when it
comes to transmitting the most elementary
conversation from actuality to paper, the
result is a lamentable distortion.   Let it be
understood, then, that I am merely an instrument in the hands of Those who at the present
time have been unable to find a better;
perhaps, having more important things to do,
They have not even tried.

Be that as it may, They credit my readers
with enough sense to know that merely
because the telephone is not painted all over
with roses, the messages that come through
it are not of necessity lies and rubbish.
Therefore they need not bother themselves
as to whether I personally am a so-called
" evolved soul " or not, or whether I have
this or that spiritual qualification.   The
reason why I have been selected to write of
such weighty matters as will be dealt with
in the following pages, is that my life is so
constituted that I am in the enviable position
of being able to devote the greater part of
it to the requirements of the Adepts.   Indeed,

I find Their activities—such of them as I am permitted to follow—the most absorbing and romantic interest of my present incarnation, and I can imagine no employment so inspiring and stimulating as that of being Their metaphorical " errand boy."

Those who tread the Path of Love may suffer when their loved ones are taken from them. Those who tread the Path of Power may suffer when their power is opposed. But those who tread the Path of Wisdom find Peace, for Wisdom cannot be taken away. When Wisdom is so powerful that it sinks into the subconscious mind and wells up again into the conscious, then it gives immunity from sorrow : for its light has banished darkness from every layer of consciousness.

—JUSTIN MOREWARD HAIG.

CHAPTER I

THE DEVA INITIATE

SHORTLY after the publication of *The Initiate in the New World*, I found myself constrained to send an S.O.S. in the shape of a letter to my Guru, Justin Moreward Haig. It was not an easy letter to write, because, needless to say, I knew he was not omniscient; he could not raise the dead, nor, from his house in Boston thousands of miles away, make the unseen perceptible to one who had lost the power *to* see. For my wife, owing, we imagine, to a series of operations, had been deprived of the clairvoyance which had made psychic communication with the Master possible. This deprivation had caused her much unhappiness, which was not alleviated till we came into contact with Chris, who, by means of her own transcendental gifts, was able to illuminate the path Viola could no longer see for herself.

3

And now Chris was dead, and Viola plunged into even greater darkness than before, since to her sense of loss was added the sorrow of being debarred from using that very faculty which alone could have bridged the gulf between herself and her beloved friend.

Chris had been no ordinary friend ; she had possessed unique qualities which set her apart from the ruck of average human beings. More of the other world than of this, yet ever ready with her amazing insight and sympathy to lessen its sufferings, she had become the pivot round which our lives for several years had revolved. Her death left Viola, who had an exceptionally strong link with her, and who has followed the path of love rather than that of wisdom, inwardly heartbroken. Emotional by temperament more than philosophical, she heroically tried to suppress her grief as inconsistent with occult ideals, but only ended in making matters worse.

And so in the hope of obtaining some advice wherewith to assuage her suffering, I resolved to send that S.O.S. to my Guru. Little did I think that the consequences ensuing from so simple a resolve would provide sufficient material for a large portion of this third book.

*　　　*　　　*　　　*　　　*

As I sit writing these first few pages, my memory goes back to that apparently insignificant, middle-aged little woman who, before she passed over, played so important a part in our occult lives, and transmitted to those few capable of receiving it such a wealth of knowledge from the Masters of Wisdom. I can still picture her with her silvery white hair and contrastingly young face, not beautiful as regards feature, but rendered beautiful none the less by an expression of spiritual dulcitude. I picture her in her rather dilapidated guest-house into which drifted human wreckage of all descriptions, derelicts broken and battered in body and mind—derelicts certain not only of welcome, but in most cases of healing for their particular ill. They clamoured for her at all hours of the day ; never had she a moment to herself. I see her always in a hurry, attempting the proverbial impossibility of being everywhere at once, often exhausted and almost ceaselessly tormented by neuralgia, yet always sweet-tempered and equable, now soothing away somebody else's headache with her strangely magnetic touch, now consoling some girl in the throes of an unhappy love-affair ; at one moment solving an abstruse metaphysical problem for a painstaking student of philosophy, the next attempting to adjust the differences between some ill-assorted married couple. Even now I still continue to marvel at the almost instantaneous adaptations she was able to make to their varied and conflicting claims.

A strange rambling house it was, with its heterogeneous assortment of patients. Christabel Portman and her husband seemed incapable of closing their hospitable doors to people of whatsoever social type or standing : the measure of their need was their sole passport for admittance ; soap-manufacturers from the North, aristocrats both English and foreign, tired little school-teachers, Indian civil servants, French, Dutch, Syrians—all these and many more at one time or another had assembled and sojourned at " The Pines," that retreat which the Portmans, in conjunction with a doctor, had run for the treatment of baffling psychological complaints. Chris, with her wonderful powers, not only diagnosed the complaint, but was psychically impressed with the most suitable means to cure it. But the ill she was best at curing, as Viola always declared, was that called " heart-ache." . . .

A number of the people were theosophists, recommended there by fellow-theosophists ; others had come at the suggestion of some unconventional physician, only to find themselves puzzled and sometimes not a little shocked at being thrown amongst such a peculiarly minded crowd.

Well do I recall the incongruous snatches of conversation I so often heard at the crowded dinner-table, as the voice of one person or another predominated over the general clamour, or a sudden *piano* momentarily brought a few consecutive sentences into high relief.

" I suppose you know, Mr. Smith, that all your trouble is Karmic . . ." from an earnest and humourless spinster.

" Never 'aving coom across that word in Ma-anchester "— stolidly sarcastic from Mr. Smith — " Ah couldn't say as it wasn't. But Dr. 'Odges says it's constipa-ation."

" No, no, you don't understand—does he, Mrs. Portman ? "

" *Mais pardon, Madame* . . ." and the Frenchman's voice pierced the conversational orchestra, nasally, like a muted trumpet, " ze Absolu' can in no circomstonce evair come into manifestation—*voyons, ça n'est pas logique ça !* "

" But I've always understood from the books——"

" You can please yourselves, of course," though this Yorkshire woman did not look as if she meant it, " but give me the good old story of Jesus Christ and the Christian religion."

" None of us are denying the Christian religion, Mrs. Satterthwaite."

" Wonderful man, Sir Thomas—now he *really* manifests brotherhood."

" How that woman does love a title . . ." a whispered remark from my neighbour.

" Is the permanent atom always in the throat-centre, Mrs. Portman ? "

" Chris dear, I had such a curious dream —could it have been a memory of a past incarnation ? "

" So queer—my toes always tingle when I meditate ; do you think it means——"

" This year, next year, sometime, never——"
But this was only someone earnestly counting
her plum-stones.

And there at the head of the table sat Chris,
always the final court of appeal, at one
moment trying not to be convulsed with
laughter, at another attempting to pour oil
on troubled waters and produce a semblance
of harmony amidst the clash of so many
diverse personalities.

* * * * *

And now my memory harks back to another
and very different scene : Chris in her large
and romantic garden with its lawns and wind-
ing paths, its lily-pond, its pergolas and rose-
hung arbours ; Chris, discoursing on high
metaphysics to a small circle of men, while
they listened impressed and enthralled.
Because she never laid herself out to impress
her listeners, she never gave them the irk-
some feeling that she was " holding forth."
Moreover, if she set her mind to it and
" tuned herself in," she could give most
correct and erudite discourses on subjects
about which she had previously known
nothing. I remember an occasion on
which somebody challenged her to deliver

a little lecture on Japanese art ; she not only complied, but came off with flying colours.

Although all were agreed that " Mrs. Portman was a wonderful woman," even the theosophists, with very few exceptions, did not suspect how close was her link with those Masters of Wisdom they had been taught to revere. And had they been told, some of them would not have believed. Like Madame Blavatsky of mixed fame, Chris, from her earliest childhood, had clairvoyantly seen that impressive and love-radiating Being she later on came to know as one of the Himalayan Masters—her own special Guru. I remember her telling me one day as we sat alone together in a secluded part of the garden, how, when her body was asleep, she used to transport herself to His house in Shigatse, and with child-like rapture listen to Him improvising on the organ He had had built up there. For Master Koot Hoomi takes an especial interest in music, and endeavours to inspire all those who, in varying degrees, are receptive to His influence.

Chris had a genius for improvisation herself. She could hear the super-earthly music of the devas,[1] and, allowing for the limitations of the piano, translate it into earthly sound. It seemed strange, in a sense, that one so gifted should have been doomed to spend her life in this atmosphere of sickness and mental aberration from which I always felt that her sensitive nature inwardly shrank.

" Oh, if only I could have been a musician ! " she would sometimes rather wistfully exclaim ; then, with her funny little smile : " Ah, well, it just wasn't meant to be . . ." and as if to banish the thought, she would run off to cheer up one or other of the many patients ; when, a little later, she flitted past me again on some further errand of mercy, she flung over her shoulder : " Don't go imagining I don't love my work for my lame dogs ! "

" The more lame they are, the more you seem to love them," I retorted. Her laugh, receding in the distance, answered me . . .

*   *   *   *   *

One day I told Chris about my Guru, J. M. H., though I did not mention his name. " How frightfully interesting ! " she exclaimed, all enthusiasm ; and then that far-

[1] Nature-spirits, ranging from the smallest fairy to the highest angels.

away look came into her eyes which meant that she was " sensing up " things.

In a moment or two she smiled to herself —a whimsical, enigmatic smile.

" Now look here, Chris," I said, " you're not going to keep all that to yourself.   Strikes me, you probably know more about my Master than I do.   Come along, out with it ! "

She laughed heartily.   " How you do amuse me ! "

" Thank goodness for that ; but I'm waiting to hear what you know about my Master."

" Oh, not much ; only that his particular work seems to be in connection with preparing bodies for the new sub-race." [1]

" There you are ! " I exclaimed, " *I* never knew that."

" Oh, didn't you ? "   She was, or pretended to be, surprised.

" Well, how should I ?   He never told me. I wonder why ? "

" The ways of Masters are mysterious," she said.   " Perhaps he thought it of no importance."

---

[1] i.e. the sixth sub-race of the fifth root-race now appearing as a type in America.   The majority of mankind, born in the West, are of the fifth sub-race of the fifth root-race.

" Or perhaps he didn't want me to know, and you've gone and let the cat out of the bag," I teased her.

" He doesn't mind whether you know or not ; if he did, I shouldn't have told you."

" All right, then, please tell me some more ! "

" All these physiological Yoga practices he teaches——"

" Well, what about them ? "

" They're for the purpose of making the body extra strong and controlled, as well as extra sensitive. That's what the new Race has got to be."

" You mean that when his pupils have children, they'll inherit all that ? "

" Well, of course."

" And why specially in America ? "

" Because there are going to be a great many sixth sub-race bodies over there. But not *only* there. Your Guru, for the time being, has undertaken to do that work for the Americans in this particular cycle." [1]

[1] N.B.—The " thirty-five years' cycle of Mars," the planet astrologically responsible for wars and revolutions ; also for stimulating the study or control of the Unconscious, by means of psycho-analysis or Yoga. The cycle lasts from 1909 to 1944. See Chapter IX.

" This is getting interesting. Let's hear some more." But she was called away to deal with somebody in an epileptic seizure. Always an interruption of one sort or another.

*   *   *   *   *

I remember there were some curious people who used occasionally to turn up at " The Pines," ostensibly because they were feeling a bit " off colour," but in reality because they wanted confirmation of their own psychic impressions, or merely wished to talk about them to Chris.   One well-meaning but deluded soul was convinced that she was in frequent communication with the Virgin Mary.   On one occasion she even asked Chris to go down on her knees, as the Madonna was alleged to be present. . . .   But unfortunately all Chris could see was a mischievous spook, thoroughly enjoying the sport of masquerading as that exalted Being ; and thus found herself faced with the ticklish task of conveying to the good lady that her visions arose mostly from her own subconscious mind, or at any rate that what she saw was not quite what she imagined, and that the Virgin Mary was in no sense involved . . .

I remember another woman, stout and full-

blooded, who insisted that she got " Teachings " from Beings of quite unimaginable
altitude. These Beings, however, proved to
be strangely accommodating. The doctor had
forbidden her, for her health's sake, to indulge
a taste for port wine, but after abstaining for
a few days, she impressively informed us all
—*and* the doctor—that her " Teachers " had
overruled his injunctions ! Again Chris had
to step in . . .

She did not of course deny that the clairvoyance of such women as these was occasionally genuine. It was just the trouble, as she
pointed out, that, like all untrained clairvoyants, they could not sift the tares from
the wheat, nor prevent their " sensings " and
" seeings " from being coloured by their own
personal desires. To make people of this type
more self-critical without discouraging them
too much, was a far from easy, though quite
a large part of her work.

* * * * *

I could go on multiplying these memories
of Christabel Portman, but to do so would
be to fill the pages of a whole book. Yet
even this sketchy portrayal of her, such as it
is, has been no mere literary self-indulgence :

it has been a prelude to that most vivid of
all memories—that Sunday morning when she
came to me and said : " The Master has
offered to speak to you."

*****

In a chair alone by the fire in the little
oak-panelled room set aside for meditation,
sat Chris ; but the ineffable smile with which
she greeted me was not hers, and although the
voice was hers, the inflections and choice of
words were different.

Her lips spoke the words gently and lovingly : " Greetings, my son . . ." and her
hand held mine for a moment before motioning
me to be seated—with a gesture that was also
not hers.

And then I realized that she had done what
only initiates of an advanced degree can do
—she had consciously stepped aside, and
temporarily yielded up her body to her
Master.

Would that I were permitted to write of all
that He said on that and other occasions when
He did me the honour of speaking to me, but
He has enjoined silence. For much that He
imparted was of a private nature, and much
that He taught me may not yet be revealed

in a book. Yet of His love, His tolerance, His modesty, His wealth of language, His power to elucidate difficult problems or expound occult truths in a few simple words and a poetic simile—of these I feel impelled to speak. Despite His imposing intellect and the spirituality which radiated from Him, He seemed so endearingly human. There was none of that patronizing element of looking down from superior heights upon the childish frailties of us poor unevolved mortals. Many a time I was constrained to lament over my failures, but instead of reproaching me, He reassured and comforted me by conceding that the tasks which had been set were too difficult to be accomplished in a moment of time. As long as He saw that His pupils were really trying their best to succeed, He never reproached them ; only when they were indifferent or thoughtless did He manifest signs of displeasure.

I used to come away from those interviews refreshed and exalted in body and spirit, and with such a keenness of memory that even now I can recollect almost every word He spoke.

* * * * *

And then Chris died, and these soul-inspiring interviews came to an end.

Perpetually surrounded by patients who made ceaseless demands upon her ; always giving out and getting scarcely anything back ; expending more and more of her diminishing strength on her husband who, for years, had worked under the disabilities of an incurable malady, she herself contracted a painful and fatal disease. People had come to depend on her too much, and for the sake of their spiritual development, as well as for reasons connected with her own evolution, it was deemed best that she should be withdrawn.

Because of love, she had all her life sacrificed herself to the needs of others, as thousands of years before she had sacrificed herself to come from the free and joyous planes of the deva-kingdom to the troubled and restricted planes of earth. Although to our limited vision she was a human being, to those who could *see*, she was still a deva in spirit, and beloved of the devas as much as she loved *them*. And because of that love, the healing devas guided her hands when she touched the sick ; the sound devas inspired her when she touched the piano ; even the little nature-spirits, busy among the flowers, mingled their joyousness with that joyousness of hers, which ever radiated on all around.

CHAPTER II

SUSPENSE

The S.O.S. to my Guru was duly written, and Viola added a few lines pathetically reproaching herself for being so unphilosophical and for feeling what she knew was selfish grief. I told her these avowals were unnecessary ; all the same I inwardly admired her for being honest and not attempting to justify herself.

Strange to say, the very afternoon I posted that letter, I ran up against Toni Bland in the cloakroom of a club.

" Seems to me we've met before," he remarked.

I couldn't place him for the moment, then we both remembered simultaneously.

" Moreward Haig," said Toni, shaking hands.

He was the effeminate, mincing little man I had met many years ago at J. M. H.'s rooms, and whose camouflaged pen-portrait I had

inserted into my first book of Impressions.
I had always dreaded meeting him, lest he
should have read the book and recognized
himself.

He noticed my embarrassment and smiled.
" I *could* pick a bone with you," he said, " but
I won't. Your portrait served a very good
purpose."

Like a coward, I pretended not to understand.

" Surely you haven't forgotten your own
book ? " he suggested.

" Come," I replied, " it's bad enough to
have written the book—you can hardly expect
me to read it as well ! "

He laughed, and suddenly I began to admire
the little chap. He could have behaved so
differently, seeing how I had ridiculed him.
After that I owned up, and we had a long and
revealing talk. J. M. H. had warned me
twenty years ago not to misjudge him by
appearances ; but even so, it seemed hardly
possible that any man could change so much
for the better, and only served to show me
once again what a Guru can accomplish with
a willing pupil.

❋ ❋ ❋ ❋ ❋

A few days later I had asked Toni Bland to tea to meet my wife and Lyall Herbert, the composer, a pupil of J. M. H.'s whom I had met in Boston. We had hoped to form an exclusive trio, but who should come sailing into the room but Mrs. Saxton. This large and determined woman used to frequent " The Pines." In fact, it was I who first recommended her to go there for treatment. For some years she had been a theosophist and proclaimed herself a staunch admirer of Mrs. Besant's, a devotee of the Masters and a member of the Liberal Catholic Church. Suddenly, however, she had thrown all that overboard in favour of Krishnamurti ; and because Krishnamurti, in so many words, repudiated Theosophy, Masters and Churches of every description, so did she. . . . Mrs. Besant had at one time publicly announced that Krishnamurti was the World Teacher : very good, then ! What the World Teacher taught must of necessity be right.

Introductions having been effected, Mrs. Saxton plumped herself down, had a good look at Toni, and, as I could see, classified him at once as that effeminate, insignificant type of man she found particularly objectionable.

We had not seen her since Chris died, so I murmured something about the tragic fact of her death.

" Tragic ? " said Mrs. Saxton, and her complacently cheerful tone conveyed a rebuke. " I don't see it like that at all."

" But so many people had come to depend on her—surely——"

" They should learn to stand on their own feet," she interrupted sententiously.

" Even if they're so weak that their legs wobble ? " queried Herbert, enjoying himself.

Mrs. Saxton looked down her big nose and ignored him. " Fancy," she went on, " Miss Hart—that crazy little creature who was always hanging round Christabel—actually talks of trying to communicate with her through a spiritualistic medium ! "

" Oh, do you think——" Viola began eagerly, then, flushing, checked herself.

" Do I think she's likely to get any results ? " Mrs. Saxton completed for her. " Most certainly I do not. Poor dear Christabel—she may have had her failings—believing Masters were necessary to our progress and all that—but I'm sure wherever she may be, she's out of reach of people pandering to their own weakness by trying to get hold of her through mediums."

" Poor Miss Hart . . ." murmured Viola. She was thinking, I knew, of the neurasthenic, broken-down little school-teacher, for whom Chris had been—everything.

" Blessed are they that mourn, for they shall be comforted," Bland said quietly, and Viola threw him a grateful look.

" If people lived the Truth," Mrs. Saxton declared, " they would never *need* comfort."

" If . . ." said Toni.

" If people weren't so smug——" Viola began, but I frowned at her to shut up.

" So you've been studying Krishnamurti," said Lyall to Mrs. Saxton.

" I go to Ommen whenever there's a camp," she answered, as if she were determined to go whether there was a camp or not.

" By the way, what do *you* think of Krishnamurti and his pronouncements ? " Viola asked Toni Bland.

" An excellent corrective to spiritual spoon-feeding carried to injudicious lengths. Advaita philosophy in a modern guise, propounded by a very pure and beautiful soul."

"Then you don't think he is the World Teacher?" she pursued.

He smiled. "Do we require a World Teacher to tell us what is as old as the hills? Could we rightly apply the term Teacher to a man who told us that nobody, however exalted, can teach us anything at all?"

Mrs. Saxton glared at Toni, but as he had a habit of shutting his eyes and gently musing into space, he did not see her expression.

"Are teachers *absolutely* necessary when we want to learn the piano?" he continued. "Perhaps not. But by profiting of their greater knowledge and guidance, we can at least be saved a great deal of trouble and time."

"Wouldn't it be fun," chuckled Herbert, "if somebody alleged to be the World-Piano-Teacher came and told us that all piano-professors were only so many obstacles to our ever learning to play the piano! Can't you see the crowds of conceited folk imagining they were Paderewskis, when all they could do would be to thump the instrument to bits?"

" What a delightful muffin-dish that
is . . ." Mrs. Saxton pointedly addressed
my wife.

After she had gone, we all exchanged
glances.

" How she disliked me," said Toni with
comical plaintiveness.

" And me ! " echoed Herbert, laughing.

" So much for what Krishnamurti's teachings have done for her ! " Viola remarked
indignantly.

" That's not fair," I exclaimed ; then, turning to the others : " I've known her for years
and she's always been like that. Long ago
I induced J. M. H. to go and see her, and
afterwards I put her in my first book—
properly camouflaged, of course . . ." [1]

" You and your books . . ." murmured
Toni with a wink.

" She recognized *him* all right, but luckily
for me, she didn't recognize herself. When
she took up Theosophy, partly as the result
of reading my book, and heard about Initiates,
she bragged that she'd known one in the flesh.
Of course now that she's gone over to Krishnamurti, she's given them all the bird. Still,

[1] See *The Initiate*, Chapter XV.

it's hardly fair to blame him for her short-comings—why, she doesn't even begin to know what he's talking about ! "

" So that's that . . ." Viola said mischievously.

" Some people change their character as well as their philosophy," Bland remarked, " other people only change their philosophy." He opened his eyes and smiled.

" I think your little man's perfectly sweet," declared Viola when we were alone ; " and so clever at hitting the nail on the head—gracefully."

" And that's the man who seemed as if he couldn't say boo to a goose when I first met him ! "

" I don't believe it," she laughed, " nor would anyone else. He's the sort of person to go to when you're in trouble. As for that silly old woman, and her patronizing remarks about Chris——"

" Hoho, what price brotherhood now ? " I interrupted, teasing her.

" Brotherhood be hanged ! " she retorted. " It's not even as if her attitude were the least bit original—she's only pinched it from Krishnamurti. Just because he's said somewhere that loving the individual sooner or later means suffering, she—she——"

" Hands us out ill-digested Krishnamurti as a poultice for our pain, eh ? "

She had to laugh in spite of herself.

" The fact of the matter is—" I began, but Viola took the words out of my mouth— " that Chris's dying wasn't a tragedy for *her* : she never really loved her ! "

" Precisely.   Yet even people who did love her—why, I was devoted to her myself, as you know—but I don't take it quite as hard as you do, my dear."

" Oh, you're so much more balanced and philosophical," she cried impulsively.   " I wish I were like you, but I'm not, so there it is ! I know you're unselfishly glad that Chris is free—so am I, of course—it's just—that I do miss her so frightfully . . ."   Her voice wavered and I realized how true, even though hackneyed, were the poet's lines :

> Oh, for the touch of a vanished hand,
> And the sound of a voice that is still. . . .

They defied all intellectual argument.

" Ah, well," I said with deliberate cheerfulness, " I wonder what J. M. H. will write.   I daresay he'll give us a message from her. After all, don't you remember when my mother died Master Koot Hoomi wasn't above giving me quite a lot of news about her through Chris."

" And I loved Him all the more for it," murmured Viola, " for being so—so human. . . ." After a long brooding pause she exclaimed wistfully : " Oh, how I wish J. M. H. wasn't so far away, then we could have an answer at once."

She seemed like a drowning woman grasping for a lifebelt.

CHAPTER III

THE BLOW FALLS

SEVERAL weeks had elapsed and there was still no letter from my Guru. Had Viola's health and spirits been better, and the state of our finances less discouraging, I should have felt sorely tempted to cross the ocean and present myself at J. M. H.'s house. It was now many years since I spent those memorable months with him and his disciples in Boston, and my desire to see him again in the flesh, far from decreasing with the passage of time, had only become more intense. Often during those years I had wondered why he had never suggested that I should pay him a visit, but as Chris had so aptly observed : " The ways of Masters are mysterious. . . ." Doubtless he had had his reasons. Moreover, I had had the wonderful felicity of speaking with and receiving instructions from the Himalayan Master whom J. M. H. on several occasions

had lovingly spoken of as a much higher
Initiate than himself.   This policy of temporarily handing over a pupil to another Guru
is often adopted by the Masters of Wisdom,
for whom all such petty weaknesses as " pro-
fessional jealousy," if the term be pardoned,
are non-existent.   But of course with the
passing of Chris and the shutting-off of Viola's
psychic powers, I had again become entirely
dependent on normal means of communication
for guidance and instruction.   Small wonder,
then, that both she and I waited for J. M. H.'s
letter with unconcealed impatience.

And then one morning the blow fell.

Instead of the long-expected reply from
J. M. H., I received a letter from his secretary,
briefly telling me the Guru had disappeared.
My expression as I read the few lines must
have revealed my utter surprise and dismay.

" What on earth's gone wrong *now* ? "
demanded Viola, who had just come down
to breakfast.   There was nothing for it : I
had to tell her.   It was a dreadful moment,
for I knew what it would mean to her.   She
had lost Chris, and now she had lost her
Guru, and with him every hope.   She was a
sick woman, and in no fit state to receive such

a shock as this. Yet I was powerless to prevent it. She turned very white, said nothing, then burst into tears.

By way of trying to console her, I endeavoured to make light of the communication. " My dear," I said, putting my arms round her, " you don't for a moment suppose he's disappeared for good ? He's sure to turn up again all right. D'you imagine he'd just go off and leave all his chelas like that without a word, unless he intended to come back ? "

" We never thought the Masters would let Chris be taken from us," she sobbed, " but they did. . . . Oh, I can't bear it. Am I to lose everybody I love ? "

Suddenly I felt indignant with J. M. H. What right had he to go away like this and cause such suffering ? God knows, Viola had been a faithful chela to him the year that we were both in Boston, and she heroically sacrificed herself to obey his decrees. He must know perfectly well that she was ill now, and had lost her friend, and just at a moment like this he chose to disappear ! And what about all his other chelas ? Was he just going to leave them to suffer without any sort of explanation ? But indignant

thoughts serve no purpose, and in any case
they were no comfort to Viola ; so I banished
them as best I could.   There were other letters
waiting to be opened, and among them a bulky
envelope with the Boston postmark.   I tore
it open.

" MY DEAR BROADBENT," I read,
    " As Heddon will have written you, we've had a
fine biff in the solar plexus here.   J. M. H. has
evaporated.   Two months ago he went off, leaving
us to infer he'd be back in a few days, and we've
been sitting on our behinds waiting for him ever
since.   There's even an idea that he passed out in
a rail-wreck in California, because among the list of
killed was a Mr. J. M. Haig.   Dr. Moreton, one of
the chelas you haven't met, I think, immediately
chartered an aeroplane to go and investigate, but
the body was unrecognizable.   A good many
other bodies were in the same condition.   All they
had to go on was a new suitcase with J. M. Haig
stamped on it.   Personally I don't believe this
man was our Guru.   Initiates like him don't
have the sort of Karma that gets them killed in
rail-wrecks.   I suspect Heddon, who is J. M. H.'s
most advanced chela, knows more about the whole
business than he'll tell, but that doesn't help us
any.   Several of the other chelas say they had
a hunch J. M. H. was going to do the disappearing-
act, because just recently when he told them off
for not getting ahead as quick as they might,
he asked if they imagined he'd always be there to
put them through their paces !

Anyway, I thought I'd write and tell you, and hope you won't feel too badly about it. Besides, I wanted to let you know I shall soon be making the trip to London. A year ago my old Dad, who'd been ailing for months, died and left me most of his money. Why not blow some of it on globe-trotting? I may be a cheerful sort of guy, but gee! this has knocked some of the guts out of me. This place without J. M. H.—well, I just feel I want to get away from it for a while. Expect to sail in about a month and will give you a ring when I arrive. Remembrances to Viola.

Cordially,
ARKWRIGHT.

P.S.—Suppose *you* haven't seen a tame Guru wandering about London? "

The writer of this breezy epistle had indeed hit the nail on the head when he spoke of a biff in the solar plexus. What on earth was I to say to Viola now? She had left her breakfast untouched and gone out of the room, which at any rate gave me time to think. To tell her that perhaps J. M. H. had been killed—that would be the last straw. In her present state of mind, the mere suggestion of such a tragic possibility would be sufficient to make her believe it was true. And *was* it true? Might it not be possible that J. M. H. had still had some Karma to work off, and had chosen that way ? The thought was horrible ! He had gone on that train knowing that at a given moment the crash would come and he would be killed. Think of the ghastly anticipation. . . . Or perhaps after all he was not the advanced Initiate we had imagined him to be. Perhaps unlike the high-grade Indian Yogis of whom he so often spoke, he could not foresee the moment of his death, and even *his* remarkable clairvoyant faculties had been withdrawn from him by Powers higher than himself.

And so I who had thought I could never doubt, found myself plunged in that most desolating of all soul-states. As soon as I tried to dispel my doubts by one argument, a counter-argument would immediately spring to my mind, as if some entity were standing beside me, and impressing it upon my brain.

Meanwhile there was my wife, probably upstairs in her room, struggling in the throes of a twofold grief. I must go to her. But I decided to say nothing about this letter from Arkwright. If later on I received definite proof that J. M. H. had been killed, then I would have to break the news to her as best I could.

I found Viola lying on her couch, in pain, both physical and mental. " That poor little Miss Hart——" she began feebly.

" Yes, dear, what about her ? "

" D'you think she really has been able to communicate with Chris ? You remember what Mrs. Saxton said."

I nodded. " There's no telling," I answered encouragingly. " Are you thinking of trying yourself ? "

" I feel I'd like to see her—d'you think you could ring her up ? "

I went to the telephone. Presently I was talking to Miss Hart, or rather she did most of the talking.

" How good of you to ring up . . . I've been wanting to see you so badly, but felt too shy. . . . Are you quite sure I shan't be disturbing you if I come ? Quite sure ? And not tiring Mrs. Broadbent too much . . . ? I know she's not well, and when you're not well— I think I'd better not stay too long. Supposing I just come for a quarter of an hour ? Or is that too long ? Shall I——? "

" My God ! " I exclaimed when at last I was able to hang up the receiver.

Miss Hart came along that afternoon ; a

wistful, restless, voluble little creature of very
uncertain age, totally unmodern in every
respect. I had not intended to be present at
the interview, but got caught.

She was in a turmoil of hope, doubt, yearning and bewilderment. She sat down beside
my wife with the air of a child who wants
to tell one all about it, though, as a matter of
fact, she had started to do so long before we
could induce her to be seated.

" Such a nice woman . . . so kind . . .
only charged me five shillings for the sitting
because I mentioned I wasn't well off and have
these headaches . . . darling Chris used to
be so wonderful with them—a touch like
magic . . . Oh, dear . . . but I mustn't
depress you, Mrs. Broadbent . . . let me see,
what was I saying ? Oh, yes, this medium
. . . only five shillings . . . *wasn't* it good of
her ? And then people say mediums are just
out to make money. She described Chris—
oh, I'm sure it was Chris—her white hair,
the blue dress she used to put on in the even-
ings, the funny little ways she had, her smile
—everything . . . and she said Chris sent me
her love and said she wasn't far away really,
and "—suddenly Miss Hart's voice broke and

her eyes filled with tears—" and then Mr.
Clegg spoilt it all—and he's supposed to be
such a wonderful psychic ! "

" Spoilt it ? " Viola asked eagerly. " How
do you mean ? "

" When I told him about it afterwards—I
often meet him, you know—he said Chris was
so advanced and would have gone to such a
high plane that it would be impossible for her
to communicate ! That was only her astral
shell the medium saw—think of it, only her
astral shell—and I was so sure——"

" I should have thought," I gently interrupted the torrent, " that the more advanced
the soul, ,the more compassionate, and the
more she'd want to try and comfort those she'd
left behind."

" Oh, Mr. Broadbent," cried the pathetic
little creature, her eyes filling again, " do you
really think that ? "

" I don't see how one could think anything
else," I replied. Then I excused myself and
made my escape.

It struck me afterwards that a man like
Harold Clegg might have had more sense than
to ventilate his assumptions about Chris's
after-life to a woman like Miss Hart. Why

couldn't he have left her her morsel of comforting illusion, if illusion it was, instead of snatching it from her in that brutal manner? And now of course Viola was involved; she had often met Harold Clegg at " The Pines," and been impressed by his clairvoyance; so she would be inclined to give credence to what he had so unwisely affirmed.

And my fears proved only too correct. When Miss Hart had gone, Viola said dejectedly : " I'm afraid there's no hope *there* either . . . I'd thought for a moment—but if Harold Clegg hadn't been right about Chris, he'd have seen her himself without any medium."

" Not necessarily," I rejoined. " She liked him well enough, but there was no real link between them. Much more likely she'd appear to people who really wanted her than to a man like that who thought she'd gone to God knows where—Venus or the Pleiades. Such rot ! "

She laughed sadly. " Miss Hart wants me to go to this medium of hers. She seems to think I could tell whether it was really Chris or not. I told her I'm as blind as a bat these days, but——"

" If it'll make the little woman any happier," I interrupted, " I should go."

But it ended in my going too.

*   *   *   *   *

A queer little room it was in a rather sordid street. There was nothing eccentric about the medium who chose to call herself " Euphonia." She did not treat us to any hocus-pocus or pseudo-occult affectations. She possessed this peculiar mediumistic faculty, and was out to help us as best she could.

After relaxing in an armchair for a few minutes, she began to go through a series of contortions ; suddenly she sat bolt upright and rubbed her hands with vivacious satisfaction. Snowflake, the medium's control, had " come through "—a little Indian girl as she afterwards informed us.

Snowflake was delightful, full of jokes and quaintnesses of speech. She addressed me as " Mr. Man," and Miss Hart and Viola as " lady."

" Oo," she said, turning to Viola, " what lovely colours round your Mr. Man ; 'e ain't no cheap soul, 'e ain't . . . 'e much loved this side, 'e do big work out of body and big work in body too. . . . We known him long time,

we 'ave . . . 'e in touch with the Big Masters
—me feel like little worm——"

" Come, come," I remonstrated, " are you
out to make me blush, or what ? "

She went off into peals of laughter. " Aha,
if oo 'ad dark skin like me, oo couldn't blush ! "
Then all at once she became serious. " Ah,
lady, oo also beautiful aura, but what sadness
—oo 'ave suffered much—me feel all weepy
. . . and other lady too—always so sad, so
sad—dear friend Snowflake see before—white
hair, blue dress, lovely smile—she come over
this side and leave much sadness—but never
mind . . ." rubbing her hands, " me and my
meedie, we see what we can do." She paused
and cogitated for a few moments, then :
" Beautiful little lady here now—says she will
try and control meedie—but," shaking her
head, " very difficult—very difficult—little
lady very big soul—vibrations too quick for
poor little meedie. But we will try, we will
try—Snowflake help. . . ." The medium
sank back in the chair and was motionless
for a while.

Once again she sat up ; there were no contortions this time, but her heart was beating
so rapidly that I could hear it from where I

sat.   Chris, if Chris it really was, extended
her hands with a gesture that might have been
hers, and gave one to Viola and the other to
Miss Hart.   I heard my wife catch her breath.
Then a very faint voice that was neither
Snowflake's nor the medium's own said :
" Well, here we are again. . . ."

Viola winced : Chris would never have used
such an expression.

" You thought I'd leave you high and dry "
—another expression she would never have
used—" but I couldn't do that.   You wanted
me, so I've tried to come. . . .   It's like old
times, isn't it ? "

" Chris, darling, *are* you happy ? " Miss
Hart asked, trying to control her emotion.

" So-so," she answered with a wan smile.
" I should be if they weren't all so sad."

" You mean your lame dogs ? " Viola said
softly.

She shuddered.   " It's all such a sticky
mess ! "

Viola winced again, though on my part I
realized the expression referred to the turgid
state of the auras of those who grieved.

" I must go," Chris said abruptly, " the
power's giving out."   She took my hand and

pressed it. " Dear friend," she murmured,
" and I've had no time to talk to you. . . ."
The medium fell back in her chair.

Viola came away from the sitting depressed
and exhausted. Emotionally, more especially
during the first few moments when Chris had
appeared to take control, she had been convinced ; but intellectually she was repelled by
what seemed a vulgar travesty of our friend.

" Those dreadful expressions——" she reminded me.

Yet drawn by the hope of getting better
results, she went to the medium again and
again. A sense of almost overwhelming love
was always conveyed, but when this came to
be expressed either in Snowflake's quaint
borrowed phraseology or that of the medium
herself, the effect jarred.

" It's so tantalizing . . ." Viola confessed
to me, " Chris—and yet not Chris . . . Chris
all muffled by the medium's personality. . . ."

We never got anything really convincing or
illuminating as to our friend's life and
activities on the other planes ; in fact, far
from giving any impression of their joyfulness
and beauty, she seemed rather to be swamped
by the darkness and sorrow of earth-conditions

which she perforce contacted when she made the sacrifice of descending into denser matter to control the medium. That it *was* a sacrifice, Viola by degrees became convinced. Although Chris apparently made heroic attempts to maintain the link she had established for the sake of her sorrowing friends, she grew increasingly less like her true self, as if she were receding to greater and greater distance ; until at last Viola, feeling it was no longer justifiable to call her back from those spheres where doubtless all *was* joy, gradually came to renounce the sittings altogether.

Some while later, however, Euphonia rang Viola up, entreating her to go and see her, as, in her own words, she was " properly up against it . . ." In several cases where she had been most eager to give help, she—or rather Snowflake working through her—had failed dismally. Guidance volunteered had led to increased confusion ; prophecies made had never been fulfilled. Poor Euphonia, an essentially truth-loving person, was in a desperate state of mind. Was she, then, nothing but an unconscious and involuntary fraud ? She herself was unaware of what was said when Snowflake was in control, yet naturally she felt responsible for what " came through " ; and if her gift, such as it might be, was only to be used for trickery and to let people down—— In short, would Viola, one of her most sympathetic clients, do her the favour of having a sitting with her ; she wasn't to dream of paying for it, although poor Euphonia owned to being " on the rocks . . ." All she craved was this chance to test her powers and reassure herself that they had not entirely deserted her. " If Snowflake can't do anything for *you*," added the medium, " she can't do anything for anyone, and I may as well shut up shop."

Viola consented to see her readily enough. " I can just imagine the sort of hell the poor creature's having," she said.

" Perhaps as you're going in a purely unselfish spirit," I teased her, " you may get something through that's really worth while."

She shrugged her shoulders and laughed. " I've given up all hope ; but I can't let Euphonia down : she's done whatever was in her power for me."

Suddenly I had a brain-wave : why not get someone who could *see* to join the sitting ?

There was Harold Clegg. Although his pronouncements might not always be accurate,
he probably possessed sufficient clairvoyant
power to be able to help the poor woman in
her distress. Also why not have the sitting
in the more congenial atmosphere of our own
house, and perhaps ask Lyall Herbert to come
and send the medium " off " with a little
music. . . .

*   *   *   *   *

Lyall Herbert had played the Good Friday
music from *Parsifal* ; the medium had gone
into trance, and Snowflake took control.

" Oo," she began, rubbing her hands as
usual, " what lovely music, and what lovely
atmospheres in this 'ouse—me not afraid 'ere.
. . . And three mens—me much gratified. . . ." Then she began to moan. " Oh,
but my poor meedie, she very sad, she 'ave
'ad bad punch in tummy—me 'ave told wrong
tings to Mrs. Lady and Mr. Man who meedie
knows, and Mrs. Lady and Mr. Man very
angry. . . . We 'ave tried to tell truth, but
sometimes not easy—such a lot of astral dust,
make everything so dark, we can't see . . .
and sometimes guides 'ave let me make
mistake on purpose for sake of ee-volution of

Lady and Man. . . . But now please you tell my meedie she no fraud—she no worry any more. . . ."

I then asked her, as indeed during the earlier sittings Viola had often asked her before, if she could give us any news of J. M. H. Had he really been killed, and if not, where was he and why had he disappeared ? But she only shook her head and said that even on " their side " they were not allowed to know everything. She went on to inform us in her own quaint fashion that the elevated vibrations produced by the music Herbert had played had made it possible for the " little blue lady," as she called Chris, to come for a short while. Even in the half-light I could see the look of unselfish pleasure on Herbert's face, and the mingled surprise and yearning on Viola's. But Chris, when she did take control, though she seemed to radiate her love all around, spoke in a voice that was no more than a breathless whisper.

" I shan't always speak through this medium—I'm searching and searching everywhere . . . someone else to be a link between us—I came to tell you——" She faded out. . . .

" Well, what did you make of it ? " we asked Clegg when the medium had gone.

" Snowflake is certainly right," he replied ; " the astral conditions are so churned up these days that it makes all psychic work very difficult. I daresay a good many mediums of Euphonia's type find themselves in the same straits."

" Still, I think we managed to patch up her self-respect a bit by giving her Snowflake's messages," said Viola.

" She looked a darned sight happier than when she arrived," declared Herbert, and we all agreed.

" While Herbert was playing," Clegg continued to give us his impressions, " I saw the amusing little Indian girl hovering about the medium. Then suddenly—puff !—and she disappeared into her heart-centre like a bit of smoke sucked up the chimney."

" But what about Chris ? " Viola asked eagerly.

" During Snowflake's conversation, I saw her appear—— Oh, it was Mrs. Portman all right "—Clegg had never called her by her Christian name, "—she stood a little distance away by the wall."

" I thought you said," I began, " that she had gone to such a high——" But Viola motioned to me not to interrupt.

" When the little Indian creature withdrew, Mrs. Portman tried to control the medium's aura and sort of impress her thoughts upon it ; but she never took entire control of Euphonia's body as Snowflake did. I don't think she would have been able to. She seemed to find it hard enough to do what she was doing, and had to be helped by Snowflake. The whole thing was in a sense a mixture of Mrs. Portman, the medium and her little guide."

" That's exactly what I've always felt," Viola exclaimed, " all Chris's wonderful affection—and then when she tries to put it into words——"

" Like trying to play the piano with thick gloves on . . ." Lyall suggested, drawing his long fingers down the side of his sensitive Chopinesque face — a little characteristic gesture of his.

" That's the very simile I've wanted and couldn't find," said Viola.

" I always think it's a pity," Clegg observed, " that mediums aren't more enterprising ;

they have this gift, but they don't study scientific occultism. That good woman didn't know what was really happening."

" And you were a bit out yourself the other day, old man . . ." I was determined to have my little say. " Who was it who said Chris had gone so far that communication was impossible ? "

He laughed apologetically. " I was using my brain instead of my psychic faculties."

" Brains can be very misleading things," Herbert put in dryly.

" You nearly broke Miss Hart's heart," I said, not meaning to make a pun ; but being such a poor psychologist, Clegg didn't understand.

" That's just the trouble with some people who *can* see : they can't put themselves in the position of those who can't . . ." Viola remarked when he had left. Then rather wistfully : " I say, I do wonder who this new link will be, that Chris spoke of finding for us. . . ."

CHAPTER IV

BUT I have forestalled the sequence of events.

On the day I received the momentous letter from Arkwright, I rang up Toni Bland and Lyall Herbert, asking them to come and see me ; I felt constrained to break the news to them in case they had not received it direct from one of the chelas.

Lyall Herbert was visibly affected when I read them Arkwright's communication ; Toni, on the other hand, after the first momentary shock, closed his eyes according to his usual habit, and at once endeavoured to reassure us.

" After all," he mused, " a Master remains a Master whether he temporarily loses his physical body or not."

" But a Master doesn't go and get himself killed in that sort of way," Lyall objected. " It's one thing to allow yourself to be crucified in a great cause, and quite another to lose a perfectly good physical body in a railway accident."

" Aren't you assuming the worst before we know it is an actual fact ? " Toni queried.

" I really don't know what to make of it," I declared; " the whole affair baffles me completely. When I read that letter, I don't mind telling you fellows that the first thing I did was to begin to doubt."

" Doubt what ? " asked Toni.

" Well—I wondered if J. M. H. was quite all we'd thought he was ! "

" I feel a bit like that myself," said Lyall, " though I'm rather ashamed to own it."

Toni smiled. " Might it not be a question of Cycles ? " he suggested.

We did not follow him.

" You remember the Adept known as the Comte de St. Germain, just before the French Revolution ? " Toni pursued.

I nodded.

" After working in Paris and even mixing in society as, at one time, J. M. H. used to do in London, didn't he mysteriously disappear ? "

" That's true enough," Herbert conceded.

" Yes, but why ? " Toni went on. " I have

an idea it's because Adepts work in Cycles, and when a particular Cycle comes to an end, they need to alter their policy and make all sorts of adjustments." He opened his eyes and looked at me. " Wasn't it around 1908 that J. M. H. disappeared from London ? "

" Approximately," I agreed.

" And it was about twelve years before we saw him again in America—I arrived there a few months after you'd left, Broadbent. Did J. M. H. ever tell us what he'd been doing all that time ? "

" He certainly never told *me*," I replied. " He seemed pretty well installed there with his circle of chelas when I arrived, but how long he'd been there already he never let on."

" Well, d'you suppose he'll ever turn up again ? " Lyall asked. " That's what *I* care about. I've been sweating away in these hard times to save up enough money to go back to Boston, and now——" He broke off and I realized what he was feeling.

" But has he ever suggested it ? " Toni asked with a smile.

" No, now I come to think of it, he hasn't ! "

Toni shook his head. " It's a dangerous

thing to make plans of that sort where a
Guru is concerned. When J. M. H. wrote
and invited me to Boston, specifying the exact
time, in my eagerness I cabled asking if I
couldn't come a month sooner. The answer
was a curt, unequivocal *No* without any
explanation. When I arrived eventually, he
reproached me for sending that cable. Since
then I've learnt my lesson."

"And yet, if you please," I pointed out,
"I get lots of letters asking me to arrange
meetings with J. M. H. when even we, his
pupils, can't go and see him a minute sooner
than he chooses. On one occasion I ventured
to send him a letter from a very persistent
correspondent, and he replied : ' My son, I
thought you'd have sufficient intelligence to
realize that I can be of no assistance to a
woman so preoccupied with her own importance. . . .' That was a nasty one, though
very much to the point."

"And now nobody can get at him," Lyall
ruminated with some bitterness ; " I must say,
I think it's damned hard on all his chelas. If
he hasn't been killed, he might at least have
contradicted the rumour—somehow—instead
of leaving everyone to suffer like this.

It seems very strange behaviour for an Adept."

" Strange or not," said Bland, speaking quite emphatically for him, " there's one thing we must certainly *not* do, and that is allow all these speculations to involve us in a useless and isolating condition of doubt. Whether dead or alive, *spiritually* J. M. H. will never cut himself off from us ; but we shall cut ourselves off from him if we start losing faith the very moment he does something we can't account for. Remember, *doubt* erects a barrier that even a Master is not allowed, or possibly may not be able, to break down."

After that I more or less tacitly resolved I would be loyal to our Guru whatever happened, and I believe Herbert made a similar resolve. As for Toni's attitude, the question of doubt did not seem to trouble him greatly, or so it appeared on the surface. But then, much as I had grown to like and admire him, there was still something about him which mystified me. In any case the shock we had sustained—and only those who have been in personal contact with a Guru can realize what it meant—served to draw the three of us closer together, and our inclination was to meet more and more frequently and talk of him who had been so much to us.

* * * * *

Several weeks had gone by, and Arkwright, the breezy American chela who figured in my second book of Impressions, had arrived in England and was staying in our house. Naturally one of the first questions I put to him related to J. M. H.—was there any further news ?

" Not a particle ! " he replied.

" Yet *you* personally still think he's not been killed ? "

" Sometimes I do and sometimes I don't. What makes it look queer is that nothing seems to be known about the guy who got smashed up ; no friends or relatives went along to identify him. Dr. Moreton made every possible sort of inquiry."

I then asked how the chelas had reacted to their loss.

" Some proved what damn fine natures they were," he declared generously ; " just because J. M. H. wasn't on the spot, they really set to and got a move on. Others——" He shrugged his shoulders. " Trouble with us over there is that we're so darned hot on per-

sonalities that if a fellow comes along with
five cents' worth of magnetism and a new
stunt, we run after him like a lot of kids after
candy. I've a strong suspicion J. M. H.
tipped Heddon the wink to carry on the work
after he'd gone, but because he hasn't the
personality, some of the chelas, especially the
women, won't tune in with the scheme.
Gosh, as *you* know, J. M. H. gave us enough
teaching to last a lifetime if we'd really
wanted to put it into practice. But the idea
of keeping the centre going as a place for
study and mutual encouragement hasn't
appealed to everyone, so our numbers have
already decreased." He paused for a moment
to light a cigarette. " One or two of the
women transferred to self-appointed Vedantic
Swamis, others beat it off to California, to
see if that fellow Krishnamurti had anything
to give them. Maybe you've heard of him,
maybe not. . . . Anyway——" But here
my young son burst into the room, and in
another moment Arkwright was behaving
like a schoolboy in playtime.

I never divined why Mrs. Saxton felt it
encumbent upon her to drop in on us from

time to time, unless it was the irresistible pull of her power-complex exercised at the expense of my unfortunate wife. However, on this occasion, as it appeared, she had come with a more specific purpose than that of merely ventilating her superior opinions for our benefit.

" Not a very pleasant day," she remarked platitudinously to Arkwright, after shaking hands with him.

" Well, I guess this bum climate of yours is somewhat notorious," he replied genially, " so I'm only getting what I anticipated."

Mrs. Saxton's expression conveyed that, like Queen Victoria, she was " not amused," but she said nothing.

I intimated by way of easing the situation that she was interested in philosophy.

" Ah, that's the goods ! " exclaimed Arkwright. " Gee ! We need it these days when religion's gone to pot and our girls are pickled in alcohol and sleep with a different fellow every night, and altogether the old world's in a hell of a mess." He looked at Mrs. Saxton with an expression so disarming and friendly, that if she had been less hard and less shock-able, she would have warmed to him at once.

" I perceive the depressing state of the world has neither damped your enthusiasm nor your spirits," I laughed.

" I reckon I'm pretty much the same old codger—it takes a lot to jigger *me* up."

" What I really came for," Mrs. Saxton portentously addressed Viola, " was to offer you a ticket for Krishnaji's lecture to-morrow evening. I bought it weeks ago for Miss Hart —thought it would do her so much good, if only she could take it in, poor thing—but now—most tiresome—she's gone and got bronchitis."

" Oh, what a shame," cried Viola sympathetically ; but Mrs. Saxton somehow seemed to regard it as scandalous rather than regrettable.

" So Viola is to be done good to instead . . ." I thought to myself.

" You'll use the ticket, of course ! " Mrs. Saxton gave the impression that Viola must consider herself fortunate in thus having the chance to be liberated from the various doctrinal superstitions in which she was plunged.

" I'll be delighted to use it," Viola assented. " I've read his funny little yellow magazine, but never actually heard him lecture."

" It'll alter your whole point of view," Mrs. Saxton severely informed her.

" So Krishnamurti's here," said Arkwright. " Why, that's the guy who . . ."

" Guy ? ! " Mrs. Saxton interrupted, swelling with indignation ; " he has a most *beautiful* face."

I explained to her that in America the word was neither associated with effigies nor fireworks, but she did not appear to believe me.

Arkwright laughed heartily at his own *faux pas*, and told her he had had no intention whatever of offending her susceptibilities. " A fine fellow," he added with genuine admiration. " Heard him lecture back home. Oriental philosophy in occidental dress. As you say, a beautiful face. A bit too fond of repeating himself, though—and when a fellow repeats himself *too* much, one's nerves get kind of on the bum."

And that finished Mrs. Saxton, who made a hasty retreat.

" I guess if she never sees me again, it's too soon ! " chuckled Arkwright when she had made her exit.

But I assured him that Toni Bland and others had fared similarly at her hands.

" She seems to regard any sort of human contact as an obstacle to liberation . . ." my wife observed.

Oh Krishnaji! You led us all to believe in 1926 that we were seeking happiness, in 1927 liberation, in 1928 truth, and in 1929 uniqueness; in 1930 you shattered our beliefs in reincarnation, masters, saviours, and now you speak of the removal of the " I," of the ego, of a state without birth and death, of life which seems to have a meaning to you, but not to us. And yet you speak of an attainment, of a realization, of a culmination. Has your realization, then, a progressive character— progressive in the sense that you have much to say and so your message is now passing through a state of incompleteness to completeness?

—" *Star Bulletin,*" *September,* 1931.

CHAPTER V

KRISHNAMURTI : A PROBLEM

VIOLA had gone to Krishnamurti's lecture
and we were a male quartet : Toni Bland,
Lyall Herbert, Arkwright and myself. We
had lingered over the dinner-table, and having
adjourned to the drawing-room, had induced
Lyall to play us a little Scriabine. He had
just got up from the piano when Viola
returned.

We were of course anxious to know what
she had thought of the lecture, and I jestingly
inquired if she'd been converted and become
a devotee.

She laughed. " No ; I'm only an interested
spectator. The female devotees seem to be
either those who yearn to be a mother to
him, or, enamoured of his eyebrows and
exquisite appearance, who yearn to be something quite different. . . . Then there's the
vast host of Indeterminates, trying, in spite

of inadequate mental equipment, to grapple with the negativeness of his teaching."

" Do you really find it so negative ? " Lyall asked.

" Well, for me, he's simply the Apostle of Negation," she replied, " just as Chris was the Apostle of Joy. . . . Besides, he's such a contradiction : tells people they must think for themselves—splendid, that, up to a point—and then bars all the avenues of individual thought. We're told we can't reach the goal through worship or art or beauty or help from the Masters or cere-monies : why on earth not ? Krishnamurti may not need any of these things himself, but what about others ? Surely if *they* choose to seek God through beauty or art or whatever it may be . . . ? Why, all the old religions and philosophies (which he doesn't seem to have studied, by the way, or if he has, he's chucked them into the dust-bin with the rest) . . . every teacher from time immemorial has implied that by whatever path Man tries to reach God, he gets to Him ! But Krishnamurti not only destroys the path —or paths—but the goal itself. To begin with, you're not to use the word ' God ' . . .

Krishnamurti's Ultimate Reality is just a hazy abstraction, sometimes called ' Life,' sometimes ' Truth,' but never conveying any sense of wonder or delight."

" Ah, you dear ladies," said Arkwright, smiling, " you never were dead struck on abstractions—it's part of your psychology. What you want is a nice personal fatherly God on a nice fat gold cloud, who'll hand out gallons of rich juicy comfort whenever you shout for it."

" That's not what I want at all!" she laughed. " But you must admit that whether you're a Dualist and want a God outside and beyond yourself to reach out to and worship, or you're a Monist and want to realize yourself as the One Self, reason, let alone the heart, demands a goal that's *attractive*, to say the least! You may think it's cowardly and feeble not to want to stand on a bleak mountain-top, stripped of everything, in an icy gale, while you contemplate a void—but I ask is it worth while? If this ' Completeness ' of Krishnamurti's is meant to be synonymous with happiness, what a pallid, puny thing it seems beside the joy that Chris spoke of—and *lived*. . . . She didn't anthropomorphize God ; she put the idea of Him beyond the farthest reach of thought, but only to show that all beauty and magic and mystery were just glimpses or reflections of a Reality too marvellous to be contemplated unveiled . . .   The Master who spoke through her revealed Him as the transcendent Loveliness and Lovableness for which everybody yearns, whether he's conscious of it or not, each in his own terms—and Who responds to each in the terms of his own need.   He said : *Human intellect can no more understand the Absolute, than the insect under the floor can understand a Master, but this you may know, that He is all Love . . . and that Love is the reason for the universe, the reason for your very existence !* "

" But Krishnamurti doesn't deny love—at one time he was always talking about it," I objected.

" Ah, at one time, perhaps—but not so much now ; and even when he does, the love he speaks of strikes one as so impersonal and vague as to be almost afraid of itself.   What a different sort of feeling one had when Master Koot Hoomi said : *The love that I feel for each one of you, that is God. . . .*   And again :

*Love and Truth are the keynotes of the universe
—and Love is Truth and Truth is Love* . . .
that's not much like Krishnamurti's : *Truth
can bring no comfort.* . . . How can you
reconcile the two points of view ? "

" Do you particularly want to ? " asked
Lyall.

" *I* don't, personally, Fifty Krishnamurtis
couldn't biff the idea of the Masters that we
got from Chris, and before that from J. M. H.
. . . I'm thinking of the poor wretches who
were trained on similar lines, perhaps, but
may not have quite our bulldog tenacity for
holding on. They've been taught, too, that
the Masters are their Elder Brothers, lovingly
trying to guide them into ' union with the
Infinite at ever higher and higher levels . . .'
as old Leadbeater says somewhere. And
then Krishnamurti comes along and tells
them that Masters are only crutches ; so
they chuck away their crutches, totter a few
steps, perhaps, in search of his ' Liberation,'
and fall to the ground.   Does he offer to give
them wings instead of crutches, or even to
show them how to grow wings for themselves ?
Not he ! He isn't enough of a psychologist
to tell them where to begin.   He'd prescribe

the same recipe all round : *What I have done,
you can do.* . . .   No account taken of individual limitations of Karma or grades of
evolution or anything.   Chris—she knew that
no two people can be handled the same way ;
that was the secret of her success with individuals ; *she* never handed out castor oil
indiscriminately to the whole class."

We had to laugh, but Viola, pacing up and
down the room in her boyish fashion, was full
of the indignant sympathy which the lecture
seemed to have aroused in her.

" It's all very well to laugh. . . .   I daresay it *is* good to force people to stand on their
own feet and do their own thinking," she
pursued.   " But how many of those who've
listened for so long to the voice of Authority
booming at them from the T.S.[1] are capable
either of individualistic thought, or have got
the discrimination to sift the grain from the
chaff in Krishnamurti's teaching ?   You
should have seen the expressions on some of
their faces at the lecture, as they tried so hard
and so conscientiously to follow the World
Teacher to his austere heights of glory, and
found—at any rate if they were honest with

[1] T.S. stands for Theosophical Society.

themselves—that there wasn't any glory there for *them*—only emptiness ! You could see from the baffled look in their eyes the hell they're going through—especially those women. He's taken everything from them— reincarnation, survival, meetings with their loved ones after death, the Masters' help and compassion—why, the whole spiritual struc- ture of their lives—and given them nothing in return but a nebulous state of conscious- ness that doesn't make the slightest appeal to the heart or the imagination."

" I can't entirely agree——" I began, but she ignored me, and continued to champion those whom she evidently considered were the greatest sufferers.

" They're floundering hopelessly in the void, poor things ! Too docile and obedient to deny Krishnamurti completely and stand for the old ideals ; quite unable to grasp what he's driving at and get any real satisfaction from it ; and lacking the initiative to strike out on lines of their own. . . . They're wondering if what they were taught before was only a lovely fiction : that's the spectre they have to face in their sleepless nights, and a pretty ghastly one it is, too. Nothing more devastating than to tell a person that what he believes isn't true.   Even a man who only believes in *himself* goes to bits when that belief's shaken. . . .   If the early teaching *was* a fiction, what are they to do now ? Krishnamurti has destroyed all their old landmarks ; if they venture to use or to think in any of the old terms, they get rapped over the knuckles.   They cry to him in the hope that he's still got something up his sleeve—something still unexpressed in his teaching that'll allow them to reconcile the old with the new—and they're frustrated at every turn : what's to become of them ? "

" Someone else will probably turn up," suggested Bland, " who'll try and restore their belief in the Masters."

" It may be too late : perhaps they won't be able to respond.   They'll be too battered, some of them too old.   You can't shatter the beliefs of years without damaging the very power of belief in itself—I feel pretty certain of that.   Sometimes I wonder if even the Masters Themselves don't feel a little sad when they see the gulf Krishnamurti has put between Them and those whose footsteps They were once able to guide. . . .   And now," she added with a sudden change of mood, " having talked your heads off, I'm for a sandwich ! " She waved to us ironically and went out.

" I guess friend Krishnamurti's tickled her up some," said our American, sympathetic though a trifle amused.

" So it would seem," I assented.

" Well, when you've just lost your Guru *and* your dearest friend," Herbert protested, " it's not exactly the moment to go and hear Krishnamurti belittling both Masters and personal survival."

" Yes, but what none of you realize," Toni said gravely, " is that although Viola may have lost her clairvoyant faculties, she's very mediumistic. Mentally sensitive to surrounding conditions, she is impelled to express the collective thoughts and feelings of those unfortunate women who cannot or dare not express them for themselves."

" Good for you ! " Arkwright concurred.

" Personally, I've always taken a particular interest in Krishnamurti's development," I remarked. " That he should have started as a Dualist and then become a Vedantic Monist or Advaitist, is most intriguing. Pity he's watered down his Advaitism, though, instead of going the whole hog. Merely to tell us that Truth is happiness, or even eternal happiness, isn't enough. The real Advaitist says that Truth is the Absolute-Existence-Knowledge-Bliss——"

" Ah, if he'd said that," Toni broke in, " the whole impression might have been very different. But to say, for instance, *Truth can bring no comfort* without at once qualifying the statement, is simply to upset people and leave them dissatisfied. He who knows himself to *be* that Absolute Bliss doesn't *need* consolation, and that's the whole point ! "

" I wonder," mused Lyall, " if he realizes it *is* Advaita he's teaching ? "

" Search me ! " from Arkwright.

" He seems so afraid," Lyall elaborated, " of people finding any point of contact between *his* philosophy and their own beliefs, that I'm a bit doubtful."

" Whether he realizes it or not, the fact remains," I said, " as I can easily prove to you." I took up the little pile of *Star Bulletins* I had collected, and chanced to alight on some of the very sentiments which had roused my wife's indignation. " Listen to this :

" Spiritual attainment does not lie in the following of another, whether leader or teacher or prophet . . . That following of another is a weakness . . . A mediator is but a crutch . . . Truth does not lie in distinctions, in societies, in orders, in churches. . . .

* * * * *

" As I am free of traditions and beliefs, I would set other people free from those beliefs, dogmas, creeds and religions which condition life."

I went to my bookshelf and got down Vivekananda's lectures on Vedanta, and read out :

" Nothing makes us so moral as Monism . . . When we have nobody to grope towards, nobody to lay all our blame upon, when we have neither a devil nor a personal God to lay all our evils upon —then we shall rise to our highest and best . . . Pilgrimages and books and the Vedas and ceremonials can never bind me . . . I am the Blissful One."

I turned again to the yellow magazines, and read further passages :

" . . . The ' I ' is the limitation of separateness . . . by continual concentrated effort, every moment of the day, you must remove this wall of limitation, and thus establish yourself in true freedom of consciousness. That is immortality

. . . That is to be beyond time and space, beyond birth and death. . . ."

I reverted once more to Vivekananda :

" Hear day and night that you are that soul (or One Self). Repeat it till it enters into your very veins . . . let the whole body be full of that one idea—' I am the birthless, deathless, blissful, ever-glorious Soul.' "

After that we compared numerous other passages. For instance : *I maintain that man is fundamentally free* (Krishnamurti). *We are free—this idea of bondage is but an illusion* (Vivekananda). *Happiness lies in the extreme of detachment* (Krishnamurti). *Be not attached* (Vivekananda). And so on and so forth.

" Well, I guess that's pretty conclusive," said Arkwright at length.

" The trouble is," Lyall contributed, " that Krishnamurti hasn't the knack of really getting his ideas across. He may know what he means himself, but doesn't convey it to others. I'm afraid only people who've been properly taught by a Guru beforehand can really grasp what he's talking about."

" Pre-cisely," said Arkwright. " The rest of them comprehend the knocking-down process right enough, but when it comes to what he's handing them out in place of it, it's a very different proposition. *We* know what he's after because we've studied Advaita with J. M. H."

" Who also said—don't forget," I insisted, " that it was not a suitable philosophy to be broadcast as the only means to Liberation."

CHAPTER VI

" A PIONEER OF THE NEW MORALITY "

WRITING books of this kind in which certain unconventional teachings are put forward, and in which real people are involved, may let one in for embarrassing complications.

Many years ago I had a sentimental friendship for a girl named Gertrude Wilton. Her father was an Archdeacon whom J. M. H. had been instrumental in helping : he had, in fact, been present at his death-bed.[1] Because of all he had done for her father and herself, Gertrude loved J. M. H. with the devotion one feels towards a Guru, though it was only later on that she came to realize the full significance of the term. At twenty-three she was a beautiful girl, but as a woman nearing middle age, she is, to my mind, more beautiful still. After her father's death she married a well-known barrister, and the three of us have

[1] See *The Initiate*, Chapter IX.

always been close friends. For many years Gertrude and her husband were supremely happy, though, if the truth be known, Alfred —for by that name I will call him—loved her rather more than she him.

Then one evening I dined with them and noticed that there was something amiss. Gertrude seemed ill-at-ease, and Alfred looked depressed. I knew them well enough to ask point-blank what had gone wrong, but it was so evident from their non-committal replies that they did not wish to confide in me, that I took the hint and changed the subject.

But I was mistaken : far from not wishing to confide in me, they not only in turn made me a living target for their confidences, but set me up as a court of appeal as well.

Alfred and I sat together over our cigars.

He cleared his throat. " Of course I never knew that Guru of yours, but he's had a great influence on Gertrude—I may even say on me too, indirectly."

I wondered what was coming, but having no particular rejoinder handy, waited.

" Hm," he mused, as if trying to find the right words. " You asked if there was anything wrong. . . . Well, yes, there is. I'm not a jealous man by nature. I agree with your Guru—that sort of thing's undignified and childish. But I strongly object to my wife taking up with a rotter, and making herself conspicuous all over London. Why, he even borrows money from her."

I agreed that that *was* a bit thick.

" She not only expects me to swallow my private feelings on the subject—and of course I must own to a few natural instincts which defy all theories, even though I've done my best to fight against them—but she doesn't take my point of view into account in the least. It's not that I want to stand in the way of her happiness, but after all, I have got my position to consider ! If only she'd be discreet . . . But she's so proud of the whole business that it has to be blazoned abroad ; thinks she's a pioneer or an exponent of the New Morality, or whatever your Guru called it."

" What's the attraction ? " I queried.

" God knows . . ." He shrugged. " As a matter of fact," he corrected himself, " he's very good-looking in an effeminate sort of way I very much dislike."

" Have you done anything about it ? " I asked.

" What *can* I do ? When I protest, she tells me to re-read those books of yours."

I made a wry face. " I'm afraid you're not the only husband who finds himself in this kind of predicament as the result of my books," I said by way of consolation. " I've had letters from others in a similar mess."

" Hm . . ." he mused, " so you have, have you ? . . . Well, there it is, and I'm damned if I know what course to pursue." He paused for a moment. " It's one thing for married people to forgive each other's peccadillos, but this is a very different matter. Your Guru— at any rate according to *my* reading of your books—never encouraged downright selfishness."

" Well, of course not . . ."

" The trouble is, she refuses to recognize that it is selfishness—talks about reforming the fellow, and all that sort of nonsense."

" How women do love the reformation-stunt ! " I laughed, but he was engrossed in his own thoughts.

Then he said tentatively : " I suppose you couldn't write to your Guru and ask him——"

" My dear fellow," I interrupted, " I only wish tò God I could, but I don't know where he is, or if he's dead or alive . . . As a matter of fact, both Viola and I have had rather a thin time of late—first of all she lost her greatest friend, and now J. M. H. has disappeared."

He expressed his sympathy, and agreed that in the circumstances of course his suggestion was useless.

" All the same," I hazarded, " if you think it's any good *my* talking to Gertrude . . . ? "

He laughed somewhat bitterly. " It's she who'll talk to *you*, if you give her half a chance ! "

I found Gertrude alone in the drawing-room.

" Isn't Alfred coming up ? " she inquired.

" He's writing letters," I explained, omitting to tell her the letters were merely a pretext to leave us alone. I sat down beside her on the chesterfield.

" I suppose he's been telling you ? " she said, but added without giving me time to reply : " I thought I understood Alfred, but evidently I don't. . . . I expected him to behave so differently ; it's as if he gave with one hand, and took away with the other."

I said nothing, resolved for the present to let her do most of the talking.

She turned to me impulsively. " I've been having a wonderful experience. . . . It *is* wonderful, you know, to be able to help some-one who's really worth while."

I smiled inwardly, having just heard that the " Someone-worth-while " was a money-borrowing rotter. " Well, don't you think it is ? " she insisted, cornering me.

I had to agree that it was.

" Basil is such a dear ! If only Alfred could see it . . ."

" All people are temporarily ' dears ' while we're in love with them," I couldn't resist saying.

" You're always so flippant, Charlie," she reproached me ; " this is really serious. He's a link from a past life—— Oh, I know he is . . . The very first moment we met—I knew it *then*. *Surely* you understand ? "

But despite her loveliness I should have understood better if she hadn't been so intense. When Gertrude gets intense, I get put off, and she knows it.

" If one felt it encumbent upon one to
erotically oblige all links from the past——"
I began dryly, but with considerable hauteur
she ignored my remark.

" Don't you see this is a chance to—well—
to live up to what J. M. H. taught ? That's
what I'm always telling Alfred. . . . If I
didn't give Basil what he feels he can't do
without, he says he'd simply have to go away ;
he wouldn't be able to stand it. . . ." But it
was evident that this inability on Basil's part
to " stand it " was a source of gratification
rather than regret.

" And supposing he did go away ? " I
suggested. " What then ? "

" Oh, you're so dense," she cried ; " must
one be so terribly explicit ? Haven't I as
good as told you that—er—spiritually . . ."
She stopped short and shrugged at my
apparent hopelessness.

" What you evidently want to tell me, my
dear, and don't quite like to," said I, coming
to her assistance, " is that you are a more
advanced soul than this man of yours, and
rather than let him go, and thus deprive him
of the inestimable spiritual advantages of
associating with you, you prefer to commit—

I mean, you prefer to be unfaithful to your
husband. And you're proud of it into the
bargain ! " I added triumphantly.

" Well, I'm only doing what J. M. H. would
have said was right," she replied, ignoring my
polysyllabic irony.

" Oh no, you're not, you're just being an
ordinary self-deluded female woman," I
laughed, and she winced. " Whatever you
may say, it's obvious that you *want* to go to
bed with this man——"

" How crude you are ! " she interpolated.

" . . . but instead of facing the fact, woman-
like you pretend to yourself and everyone else
that you've some highfalutin motive for it.
You know perfectly well that if you gave your
man the boot, it'd do him far more good than
anything else—he's that sort of chap. But
no—you prefer to get yourself talked about
all over the place, and put your husband in a
position no man of his eminence can afford to
find himself in. Surely you're not going to
tell me J. M. H. would advocate that ? "

Of course she retaliated with a cannonade
of arguments, none of which hit the mark ;
she even implied it was Alfred's own fault if
this affair caused him any suffering, and my

duty to try and convert him to *her* point of view. But I firmly stood my ground, and let her talk herself out.

" Look here," I said at length, trying to coax her into a more reasonable frame of mind, " don't be hurt at what I'm going to say, but it seems to me Alfred has a clearer conception of J. M. H.'s standpoint about these things than you have. He's been unselfish enough never to put his foot down and say once and for all the affair must stop —he's merely asked you not to broadcast it, and I agree with him." I took her hand, and though I was a bit too old to respond to her magnetism, I couldn't help inwardly sympathizing with this man, whoever he was, who had fallen such a victim to her loveliness. " I'm pretty well convinced," I pursued, " that if we were in the position to ask J. M. H., he'd say the worst flaw in the whole business was your dishonesty with yourself. Because Basil's attractions have been *plus fort que vous*, you pretend you've only responded in order to elevate him, which is sheer nonsense. . . . Then to gratify your vanity you pretend you're a pioneer of the new morality, but only make yourself ridiculous ; and finally, having behaved with undeniable selfishness towards your husband, you're annoyed because he hasn't *quite* filled the rôle for which you cast him . . . The truth is, you want your love-affair, your husband's tolerance of it, and—vicariously through me—J. M. H.'s approbation. . . . In short, my dear Gertrude," I concluded, patting her hand and laughing, " if you can't even eat *one* cake and have it, you certainly can't eat three cakes and have them all ! "

CHAPTER VII

DAVID ANRIAS : ASTROLOGER AND OCCULTIST

WE met David Anrias at the house of some friends, and have felt grateful to them ever since, for our meeting with him has proved not only very important to ourselves, but to this book also. Although Viola chaffingly calls him " the Wizard," there is nothing the least sinister about him, either in appearance or character. On the contrary, his face suggests geniality combined with a pronounced sense of humour, which becomes the more apparent the more one knows him. In fact, he is what the Germans would call *ein Original.*[1] Although his phraseology is normal enough, though pungent and graphic, when he is serious, in jocular mood his conversation is liberally and amusingly interlarded with astrological, psycho-analytical and

[1] Approx. " a unique personality."

theosophical terms, not to mention abbreviations and other waggeries.

Once having met Anrias, we saw him frequently ; he told us that he had spent many years in India, and that he used to retire for months at a time to a place in the Nilgiri Hills, where he practised meditation under the guidance of the Master whom Madame Blavatsky quaintly referred to as the Old Gentleman of the Nilgiri Hills. This Master specializes in astrology in relation to cosmic forces, and supervises and encourages the development of this science wherever possible. He apparently found Anrias' brain was of a type capable of being trained along lines similar to his own.

" You see, it's all a question of tuning-in to a particular rate of vibration," Anrias explained the *modus operandi*. " Naturally each Master has His own. But before attempting to make a contact with any of Them, it's absolutely essential to meditate on Him first, and realize Him within the heart-centre—because it's in *that* centre that you recognize Their different key-notes. When I could do that, I had to learn to still my mind, so that I could make it receptive to His, on a fairly high level."

" But can you always be certain it *is* a Master's vibration you've got on to ? Couldn't a Black[1] or other undesirable entity fake it ? " asked Viola, deeply interested.

" Impossible," he replied. " No Black can fake a vibration or sound a key-note based on love—and that's the one safeguard."

He went on to tell us that after years of practice he was able to tune-in to some of the other Masters. Finally he became so responsive to the various wave-lengths, that at times he even dispensed with the tuning-in process, and sensed Their presence whenever They chose to make a contact.

Of course as soon as my wife and I heard the word " Master," we bombarded our newly acquired friend with questions. It was then that he divulged a fact which filled us with elation. Master Koot Hoomi had telepathically requested him to make a contact with us through the friends previously mentioned. He had indeed conveyed that He wished through him immediately to establish a link with us, as we were going through a very difficult time. I may point out that Anrias, at the moment, had no knowledge of our

[1] The term "black" does not refer to race, but to the practice of white or black magic—which is not a racial description either! (Pub.)

previous association with Master K. H.
through Chris. He had merely read some
of my books ; in fact, he was in the very act
of reading one (written under my own name)
when the Master impressed the message upon
him. Anrias confided to us afterwards, however, that he did not react to it with any great
enthusiasm. " I was under atrocious aspects
at the time—Sun square Saturn included—
and really, to be called on to contact other
egos also having darks—and what with your
being on a different ray,[1] which always adds
to the complications, I couldn't help being
in resistance to the idea."

We had to laugh at his candour as well as
his phraseology.

Naturally at the very first opportunity, we
asked David if he could sense anything about
J. M. H. But although he made a few con-
jectures, he could tell us nothing definite ;
he had, in fact, the feeling that he was not
allowed to do so.

But as regards Chris, of whom Viola was
desperately anxious to have news, he told us
after a moment's silence, that he got from
her Master that, being a disciple of His, she

[1] The Seven Rays of evolution determine the different methods of
occult training.

had become one with His consciousness in the
Himalayas, instead of taking the usual heaven-
rest.

"Oh, then she *is* really happy ! " Viola
exclaimed with relief.

" The joy of being one with your Master
is unequalled by anything in the world.   But
why," David added in some astonishment,
" should you assume that she *wasn't* happy ? "

" Those messages we got through a medium
—well, they never really conveyed joy."

" That was because to communicate with
you at all, having nothing in common with
the medium, she presumably had to draw
on you, and as *you* were depressed, the
messages merely reflected your mood," David
explained ; " yet in spite of these poor results,
I gather that her compassion for those left
behind was so great that she still tried, by
means of her Deva powers, to keep in touch
with you as best she could."

After David had gone, Viola said to me :
" How grateful I am he's cleared all that up
about Chris—that takes most of the bitterness
out of it. . . ." She added after a pause :
" Well, anyhow, she *did* manage to get some-

thing sensible over through Snowflake—David must be the link Chris was looking for."

* * * * *

During that winter, David, Viola and I would often sit over the fire discussing a variety of subjects, or David would tell us of his experiences in India. I have always been puzzled about the psychology of the Indian race.

" Why is it," I asked, " that the Indians have these wonderful philosophies, and yet seem to be so shifty and squalid in many ways ? "

His explanation was very illuminating. Each race, he told us, has its special quality of development, as well as its particular limitation, and no man can entirely escape his race-influence, which is apt to affect his unconscious even when he least suspects it. The Indian possesses an inherited capacity for comprehending metaphysical thought, without making the least attempt to put it into practice in the world of facts. In the East there has always been the latent desire for the search after Truth on the part of the individual *only*, side by side with a totally different point of view with regard to business, in which the exercise of chicanery is practically taken for granted. The climate making physical pleasures all but impossible, these latter become almost purely mental, and often consist in the sheer delight of outwitting others, especially since British law-courts have become established in India. Even the poorest are prepared to gamble by going to law, in the childish hope of getting the better of someone. It never strikes these people that no occult progress is possible without a genuine love of truth and honesty adopted in daily life. And so one often sees this capacity to understand metaphysics and enjoy them, combined with a deliberately deceitful and secretive mentality.

One evening Viola asked him what were his views on the Krishnamurti problem. He knows Krishnamurti personally, and has a great affection for him.

" How would you like to have been dedicated to a most exalted and very difficult office," he replied, " before you had had time to realize your own personality and what you wanted out of life ? Can't you see what has happened ? From boyhood he was sur rounded by preconceived ideas as to his mission and teaching. Can you wonder that as he began to think for himself, he was in resistance to almost everything that was expected of him, and evolved a philosophy which was diametrically opposed to what was anticipated by the Theosophical Society ? The very fact that he deliberately avoids all T.S. terminology, when some of it might be so useful, only proves what's going on in his unconscious."

" Then I suppose it's that very reaction in his unconscious," Viola interrupted, " which accounts for the fact that when questions are asked at lectures, he seems impelled to drag in some derogatory allusion to Theosophy, whether it has any bearing on the question or not."

" Exactly. And now you realize why he rose up like Samson and tore down the pillars supporting the Temple of Theosophy, in one last terrific attempt to gain his spiritual freedom."

" Yes, but he crushed the worshippers in the process ; do you really consider *one* person's spiritual freedom worth the misery he's caused thousands of others ? " Viola challenged him.

" Ah, but you must remember it's largely these very worshippers who are responsible for his present attitude. . . ." David started to pace up and down the room—a habit of his when launched on the exposition of some interesting theme. " What I'm trying to get over to you egos is that the ceaseless conflicting demands of crowds of would-be chelas at his lectures, playing on his sensitive aura, forced him, by way of escape, into evolving the theory that both chelas and organizations were hindrances rather than essentials." He flung his cigarette-end into the fire, and paused to light a fresh one. " Lecturing in any case seems to me rather a wash-out these days. . . . After all, so many lecturers only deal out loose generalizations through it, or else make dogmatic assertions about states of consciousness which can only be experienced, never explained ; and what's more, to experience them, you must be born with the right combination of planets in certain signs and houses."

" Well, it's pretty evident *I* haven't got the right sort of combination," laughed Viola ; " Krishnamurti's philosophy is no use to me ! "

" Naturally," David replied, " it's not much use to *any* woman. In fact, only those who have practised Raja Yoga as men in past incarnations, like H. P. B. [1] and A. B.,[2] can get anything out of it at all. Anyway, as I said just now, and don't mind saying again," —he struck his right forefinger upon the palm of his powerful-looking though sensitive left hand—" this whole business of listening to other egos' lectures on Brotherhood or any other ideal can only produce superficial results, *appliquéd,* as it were, on to the audience—and which come unstuck at the first serious test ! "

" I'm sure there's a lot in what you say," I concurred, though we both had to laugh at his manner of saying it.

" Take Brotherhood, for instance," David went on, flinging himself back into a deep armchair ; " it's gassed about such a lot, but it really only results from inner experiences —not from endless talking. . . . I remember wandering casually into a little village post office in the Nilgiris one day . . ." His tone became reminiscent. " As I handed over the

[1] Short for Helena Petrovna Blavatsky.
[2] Short for Annie Besant.

money for my stamps, I recognized the official as a chela of one of the Masters. We understood each other instantly—no need for the clumsy medium of words. . . . I realized he must have exceptional clairvoyant powers, and that he'd gone through many experiences, both in and out of the body. He probably felt the same about me. . . . And there was another time, I remember, when I met a couple of Indians who had come to bring me a translation from the Sanscrit which I needed ; not a word spoken, yet through the same silent rapport, based on the same subtle source of instruction, we knew each other at once as chelas of my own Master."

We were all silent for a while, gazing into the fire, occupied with our own thoughts.

Suddenly David pulled out his watch. " Past eleven, you egos ! " he exclaimed, jumping up, " time to catch last bus home."

CHAPTER VIII

THE TELEGRAM

ARKWRIGHT, who had been joined by his wife, had departed for the Continent to continue his globe-trotting. We saw him go with regret, and gave a little farewell dinner at which Toni and Herbert were present. Toni seemed worried and preoccupied, and we wondered what was the matter with him. But a few days later I was greatly shocked to see by the newspapers that he had become involved in a most unpleasant scandal. It eventually proved to be one of those long-protracted affairs which tax a sensitive nature like Toni's to the utmost. This scandal, I think and hope, has now been forgotten, so the less said about it, the better. I would not mention it at all, did it not bear a certain occult significance which will be apparent later on.

Meanwhile, Viola and I continued to see much of David, who, in addition to his astrological activities, was studying the effects of the Cinema, about which he had obtained much valuable information from his Master. Indeed, he learned that in this particular Cycle of Mars, films were to play a very important part in the evolution and education of the masses.

" It's like this," said David in one of his waggish moods, " although pietistical egos and the gloomoids of occultism with Saturn rising "—he chuckled—" may sniff at the films as mere frivolities, the Masters take a very different view of them."

" That's where They are so wonderful and so human," exclaimed Viola ; " don't you re-member "—she turned to me—" when we took Chris to that rehearsal of a revue at the Prince of Wales's, how impressed she was ?   Why, some of those wretched ballet-girls who'd been at it for hours and hours, and were ready to drop with fatigue, had to repeat their stunts over and over again till the last super in the last line had done her bit properly, and the producer was satisfied.   Chris said she never could have believed that a mere rehearsal could be such a marvellous school for patience and self-control ! "

" Yes, and my goodness, how shocked old Miss—I forget her name—was, that Chris should want to go to a theatre at all," I added, " especially to a revue ! " I was about to continue, when we caught sight of Mrs. Saxton—we were at a restaurant at the time —and she had just wandered in with a friend. " Oh, Lord ! . . ." I exclaimed, " I hope she won't see us."

But she did, and made a beeline for our table. Fortunately she only stood a few minutes talking, then rejoined her friend elsewhere.

" Large Scorpio vehicle, Mars afflicting the ascendant," mused David, astrologically summing her up from her appearance, " semigloomoid with enormous power-complex ; upper lip seccotined to teeth, denoting firmness ; hat kept on by suction . . ."

We laughed.

" Looks as if she were having darks— vehicle heading for Crematorium. . . ."

" Now then," I protested, " none of your macabre prognostications ! "

" You wait and see. Oh, when will that low-geared waitress bring us our grub ? " He broke off, suddenly peevish. " I knew she was a Taurus, the slowest sign of the Zodiac."

" Never you mind the waitress and the Zodiac just now," said Viola firmly; " I want to hear more about those films."

But his mood had changed, and he was more interested in a couple several tables off. " Look at that thin-lipped Capricorn, sitting alone with female ego—not one word has he uttered for quite ten minutes, though he's enamoured of her vehicle."

" Perhaps that's just the reason," I suggested.

" It wouldn't be the reason if he weren't an Englishman ; now, a Frenchman—— You've no idea the difference there is in racial reactions ; I've made rather a study of them ; why——" He seemed fairly launched on what promised to be a very interesting subject, but Viola laughingly brought him back to the point.

" Those films . . ." she persisted.

David made a gesture of impatience, but suddenly we noticed on the wall a poster of a well-known film-actor. After gazing at it for a while he said with renewed interest : " Have you ever thought what a terrific astral pressure a film-star like that must be subjected to ? Just imagine the thousands of thoughts and emotions perpetually directed towards him ! Of course when he's concentrated on some work, they wouldn't affect him very much ; but when he's off guard, so to speak, or asleep and functioning in his astral body, they're apt to catch him up in a whirlpool of conflicting currents, which would be very disorganizing if he didn't know how to protect himself. Fortunately this situation was anticipated by some of the Masters, and They instituted a special course of training, by means of which film-stars could develop in a comparatively short time an intense alertness on the astral plane. I didn't get all this off my own bat," he interpolated, " I got it from my Master. In the ordinary course it would take years, if not lives, to develop this alertness, but because these film-stars are often in such a difficult position owing to their popularity, they are equally eager for the knowledge how to protect themselves. When once they've got this knowledge, it often results in their desiring still higher knowledge ; in this way they progress far quicker than if they'd just been leading ordinary humdrum lives."

" I take it they don't know anything about

all this in their ordinary waking consciousness ? " I queried.

" Not unless they happen to be very psychic —which is unlikely—and can bring the memory through in dreams."

" What planet rules films ? " Viola asked, being interested in the astrological side of the question.

" Neptune," David answered ; " it also rules drugs and mysticism."

" A queer mixture," I commented, " I can't see the connection."

" Neptune," he explained, " has to do with the world of illusion and art. Both films and art are closely associated with illusion, as anyone can see if they give the matter a moment's thought. When Greta Garbo shows herself to us on the screen, for the time being she deludes us into the belief that we actually see her in the flesh. When a painter paints a landscape, he creates the illusion that we're actually seeing that landscape."

" And drugs ? " I asked.

" Drugs also create an illusion. What price de Quincey and his opium dreams ? "

" Quite right," I assented. " But there's still mysticism to account for ! "

" The mystic has to ascend through the planes of illusion to the planes of Reality. But even Reality in the philosophical sense is an illusion from the physical standpoint— so in any case mysticism is associated with illusion in one form or another, though of course ultimate mystical truths aren't illusions."

" Jolly good explanation," Viola applauded; " all the same, it does seem queer that the same influence can make you either a mystic or a drug-fiend ! "

" Ah, but don't forget," cried David, always eager to expound his pet subject, so full of mysteries for the lay mind, " that planetary influences only create the *tendencies* to react to one thing or the other ; and how far and in what direction the individual chiefly reacts depends on his stage of evolution, and what other planetary forces are playing upon him."

" Isn't Neptune a so-called esoteric planet ? " Viola inquired further ; " I seem to remember reading something of the sort."

" Both Neptune and Uranus are, or rather used to be, esoteric planets."

" What's the difference between esoteric and exoteric ones, anyway ? " I asked.

" Well, exoteric planets are those which are in direct astral and psychic communication with the earth ; they're its guides and watchers, both moral and physical—you've got to remember that all these planets are ensouled by tremendous Spiritual Beings who wield powers greater than you can imagine. . . . Now then," he continued with emphasis, as he abstractedly but adroitly balanced a pepper-pot on the end of his knife, " Saturn, Jupiter, Mercury and Venus come under this category [1]—I mean, they influence mankind *as a whole*, whereas Uranus and Neptune, the esoteric or secret planets, could only until quite recently influence the higher vehicles of consciousness of the most advanced types. But according to Indian astrologers, a change took place on the New Moon of January, 1910 —to be quite accurate, when the Solar Logos began to take a Cosmic initiation——"

" What—d'you mean to say even the Logos takes initiations ? " I interrupted in amazement.

" So I've gathered from my Master," David rejoined.

" Good heavens . . . ! "

[1] The influence of the planet Mars will be dealt with later.

" Sounds a bit startling, I grant you ; all
the same it's an occult fact that all Spiritual
Beings in the Cosmos, whether above or below
the rank of a Solar Logos, have to go through
initiations commensurate with their particular
stage of evolution. Anyway, from then on-
wards, Neptune and Uranus became exoteric,
in the sense that they, or rather the forces
emanating from them, were drawn in to
create new magnetic currents within the Solar
System. These currents became specially
focused on our earth ; and one of the results
was that prophecies based on previous calcula-
tions proved incorrect, because Neptune and
Uranus hadn't been taken into account in
everyday affairs, and Jupiter, always looked
upon as the most powerful benefic, was still
assumed to be the predominating planetary
influence of the future. Even the Theosophical Society was misled by this assumption,
and imagined that ceremonial, among other
things ruled by Jupiter, was to play a
prominent part in their activities. The
Society's found, however, that the response
to their form of ceremonial, hasn't come up
to expectations."

" You mean the Liberal Catholic Church ? "

Viola interrupted, but David went on, ignoring her question.

" Years ago," he declared, neatly replacing the pepper-pot, " I pointed out in various T.S. journals that Neptune and Uranus were the influences to be reckoned with, and that it was useless to build on Jupiter. But needless to say, no one paid the least attention. . . ."

" I don't wonder," Viola teased him, " no one ever pays any attention to true prophets, especially when they're free-lances like you into the bargain ! "

" My dear fellow," I said, " you'll have to write a book on your astrological and other occult findings."

He gave his rather schoolboyish grin. " I've every intention of doing so—when the time is ripe."

We had left the restaurant and were walking towards Marble Arch. " Well, you egos," he remarked airily as we reached the bus stop, " here we part—to-morrow I'm off to the country for a bit."

" What—you're going to desert us ? " cried Viola, " and you spring it on us all of a sudden like this ? "

But he only chuckled to himself, and would not even tell us his destination.

" You're a queer fish," I observed, chaffing him. He had done this once before : left London for weeks on end, never written us a line, and then suddenly turned up again. When we asked him what he'd been at, he answered casually : " Oh, just meditating and things. . . ."

Viola and I were not in the best of spirits as we went home ; we were worried about poor Toni Bland, and felt for him in what he was going through ; and on top of that David was taking himself and his enlivening waggeries off to the country.

And then suddenly everything was changed in the most unexpected way. When we arrived back, there was a telegram waiting for me on the hall table. It ran :

> *Take the* 11.29 *a.m. from Paddington on Monday to* —— (a place in a south-western county was specified). *You will find a blue car waiting at station. Tell no one but your wife. J. M. H.*

" Our Guru is in England ! " I exclaimed triumphantly, as I handed the wire to my wife.

CHAPTER IX

A MASTER'S HOME

It was a Tudor house standing in the most beautifully kept grounds, with a view of wooded hills in the near distance, bright with the first foliage of spring. I was shown into a great library, and as I entered, J. M. H. was standing with his back to the fire, and an old gentleman in a skull cap was seated at a table littered with books and papers. J. M. H. advanced to greet me, with that incomparable smile of his ; then, putting his arm round my shoulder, led me to the old gentleman.

" Sir Thomas," he said, " this is one of my chelas, Charles Broadbent."

The old gentleman looked at me over the tops of his spectacles, smiled and shook hands. I gauged him to be nearly eighty, though he had but few wrinkles on his pale and powerful face.

" Sir Thomas, as you'll have gathered, is our host," J. M. H. explained.

I murmured something about his kindness in offering me hospitality.

" Tut, tut," he mumbled cheerfully, " very glad. Plenty of room in the house." He looked at J. M. H., nodded significantly, and withdrew, taking a bundle of papers with him.

After he had closed the door behind him, J. M. H. regarded me for a few moments in silence, and the love that radiated from him was a thing only to be experienced, not put into words. It caused me to feel a lump in my throat, and when at length I spoke, my voice sounded unsteady in my own ears. " I need hardly tell you what this means to me . . . especially as we thought you might even have been killed."

" You know the old saying," he answered, smiling, " that in order to be kind, one sometimes needs to be cruel. Do you think I've enjoyed being cruel ? "

" I believe there's nothing you'd enjoy less," I declared with true sincerity; " still, I'd better own up at once that when I first heard you'd gone, for a moment I was indignant even with you ! "

" That was only natural, my son ; I have no reproaches to make. But this much I'll tell you : I had no idea the Lords of Karma had decreed the death of a man with the same name and initials as myself, until it had actually occurred, and then I only sensed it from the thought-currents of my chelas."

" And yet when you did sense it——" I began, but checked myself.

" Why do you hesitate ? "

" Because although what I was going to ask was merely for the sake of information, it might have sounded like criticism."

" You may ask it all the same."

" Then why didn't you counteract the report that you were dead ? "

" Because those who believed it were foolish—and those who did not believe ,it hardly required to be told it was not true."

" Yet at one moment I believed it myself ! " I confessed.

" All the more merit, then, in ceasing to believe it."

He motioned me to an armchair, but continued to stand himself.

" Listen, my son.　You think I am my own

master—you are mistaken. I am but an instrument, however willing, in the hands of Those who have taken far higher initiations than myself. You also think that when I left my house that time in Boston, I never intended to return : you are again mistaken. If I never went back, it was because I received orders not to go back."

" But Arkwright told me you had dropped hints——" I began.

" True : because I had been warned by my Superiors that my time over there was drawing to a close, and that I should take steps, so to say, to put my house in order."

" Is that why Heddon is credited with knowing more than he'll tell ? "

He assented, looking a trifle amused.

" Would it be a legitimate question to ask *why* you had to leave America ? " I inquired tentatively.

He regarded me with those magnetic blue eyes of his. After a moment's reflection, he said : " It's an unwise mother who carries her child when it should be learning to walk ; and it's an unwise Guru who remains with his chelas when they should be learning to fend for themselves."

" And that's the only reason ? " I exclaimed in surprise.

He shook his head. " There are several reasons, my son—reasons partly connected with group-Karma, partly with the tainted magnetism of large cities—especially in the United States—and partly connected with my own development." He folded his arms across his chest, and looked down at me benignly. " When you wrote the preface to that first book of yours, you said that some of the Adepts lived in and travelled about the world like ordinary mortals. True ; but what you omitted to say was that from time to time it becomes absolutely necessary for them to go into retirement, in order to counteract the wear and tear on their physical and subtler bodies resulting from contact with their fellow-creatures. To be quite frank, psychic conditions in America are so turbulent and disintegrating at the present time, that my Chief put his foot down and refused to let me remain there any longer."

" But why should those conditions be worse in America than elsewhere ? " I asked.

" Ah, why indeed ? " He took a few paces up and down the room. " Those who make an unwanted law calculated to remove one evil arouse the desire to break that law, and the ensuing evil—or evils—may prove to be worse than the first."

" You're referring to Prohibition ? " I hazarded.

" I am. The use of alcohol is hostile to the development of those psychic and intuitional faculties which are latent in the American people. This being so, the National Devas [1] inspired this idea of Prohibition. What has been the result ? Because they are not supposed to drink, it has become fashionable for the upper classes to drink more than ever. That is one evil. Add sexual promiscuity, bribery, corruption, law-breaking and rebelliousness to that first evil, and you have several others equally, if not more disintegrating. For years I endured the obnoxious magnetism engendered by such conditions, adapting myself as best I could. I even resorted, as *you* know, to the habit of excessive smoking, in order slightly to reduce my sensitiveness, and thereby called down upon myself the censorious thought-waves

[1] High spiritual Beings helping to direct the evolution of different nations and races towards a specific end.

of fastidious Theosophists and others," he interpolated with an indulgent smile, " who read about it in your book. . . . However——"

" Oh, if I'd known that, I shouldn't have dreamt of mentioning it ! " I interrupted ; " but you did warn us, you know, about intolerance towards smoking and other comparatively harmless habits, even in your talks——"

" I am not retracting that," he retorted, dismissing with a gesture the matter as insignificant. " I'm merely explaining to you the adjustments I was forced to make." He sat down in an armchair facing me. " The time for making those adjustments is now past, and because a new Day, requiring new methods and new teaching, has dawned, I was commanded by the Great Ones to retire, in order to recuperate and train myself for the new work that is to be allotted to me."

At this juncture Sir Thomas came back into the library. " If you wish to retire to the Blue Room, here is the key," he said to J. M. H., handing it to him.

" Come," said J. M. H.

We walked the length of a long broad passage, hung with ancestral portraits, until we reached a small Gothic door.

"Enter," he said, after applying the key to the lock.

It was a small room completely bare, save for three high-backed carved oak chairs, which faced in a semicircle one of the richest and most exquisite thirteenth-century stained-glass windows I have ever seen. The walls and ceiling were blue, and on each wall was a lovely painted panel. There was a faint odour suggesting incense, though whether it was really incense, I cannot say.

"What gorgeous colours," I marvelled, "and what a wonderful atmosphere in this room." . . . He smiled agreement, pointed to one of the chairs for me, and sat down in the adjoining one.

"We are at present in the Dark Cycle," he began, "about which your astrological friend can tell you much, if you choose to ask him."

"So you know about Anrias?" I queried in surprise.

"I have cast my eye over him," he answered, smiling.

"Then how was it he didn't see *you*?"

"How d'you know he didn't?"

" Well, he never said so ! "

" Some people can keep a secret . . ." his tone was gently ironical, " which, as you know, is the A B C of occultism.   But I was telling you about the Dark Cycle,"—he changed the subject—" the Cycle in which Shiva, the Destroyer,[1] is operative.   It started in 1909 and will only end in 1944, though its influence may begin to wane before that year.   Its destructive forces were responsible for the Great War and the social upheavals which followed.   But what we are particularly concerned with, are its effects on group-psychology.   As you remember, my activities were largely centred round a group of students. For a long time I endeavoured against great difficulties to hold that group together, but finally it got beyond my control.   The group made what is termed group-Karma, in various ways not fulfilling my instructions—this you were not in a position to know—and only by dispersing that group both physically and psychically by withdrawing from it in what

---

[1] Shiva precedes action, or Brahma as desire for life, and succeeds Vishnu or knowledge as destroyer or regenerator. Shiva as desire acts and reacts, attracts and then repels. Martian types are under this aspect of the Logos.

appears to you a cruel manner, could I enable my chelas to work off that Karma through the suffering entailed." He smiled at me whimsically. " Now do you understand how cruelty may be but kindness in disguise ? "

I understood fully, and said so.

" But that is not all," he pursued ; " as the Gurus always try to kill several birds with one stone, this policy was also used as a test for the chelas—a test for their loyalty, a test for their faith, a test for their capacity to stand on their own feet. It is largely because you have survived that test, that you are here now ! "

And at that moment I realized how glad I was I had " stuck to my guns " and speedily banished those doubts I had once entertained.

But he still had something of profound interest to tell me.

" During this Dark Cycle," he went on after a pause, " the Planetary Logos, or Earth-Spirit, is throwing off and transmuting poisons just as at times human bodies throw off and transmute poisons. The result is a disturbance in the collective astral or emotional body of mankind ; and those who have not acquired control give themselves up to promiscuity, alcoholism or even criminal activities. This is what is happening now, and on such a large scale that it naturally affects the race and its development. If you ask your astrological friend, he will tell you that the influence of Mars is responsible." J. M. H. looked at his watch. " And now I must leave you, as I have some matters to attend to with our host. . . . I would suggest a stroll in the garden," he observed as he conducted me along the gallery. " We dine at eight. . . . Oh, by the way," he added, " Sir Thomas would prefer you to remain within the grounds as long as you are here."

Before I could answer, he had gone.

CHAPTER X

THE MASTER DISCOURSES

WHAT an extraordinary request, I thought, as I strolled forth into the evening air. If it had come via anybody but J. M. H., I should have felt uneasy. To be invited down to a country estate, and then be treated like a prisoner, was strange, to say the least. Who was this mysterious old gentleman, anyway? For it suddenly struck me that I did not even know his surname! Had J. M. H. withheld it on purpose when he introduced us? Then it occurred to me that I had no idea where I was. We had driven miles and miles in the car. . . . All at once I got the idea that for some reason Sir Thomas did not wish me to know the lie of the land, and therefore desired that I should remain within the grounds. Yes, but why? I gave it up, and began to speculate as to what the relationship between him and J. M. H. might be. And then my thoughts turned to J. M. H. himself. For the first time in my experience of him, he had looked a little tired, but apart from that, there was no change in his actual appearance. But his manner had changed. He had completely shaken off his assumed American characteristics, and become the J. M. H. I had first known years ago, with that slightly Victorian dignity and touch of ceremoniousness which was so charming, and which, alas, has died out in the present age. . . .

After wandering about for some time, engaged with my own reflections, I heard a bell ring : obviously the dressing-bell ; so I went to my room and changed for dinner.

*　　*　　*　　*　　*

The dining-room was oak-panelled, with valuable pictures—one by Vandyke—on the walls.

We sat down seven to dinner. Apart from Sir Thomas, J. M. H. and myself, there were three men and one elderly lady who took the head of the table opposite our host, whom, I observed, she addressed as " Uncle." Once again the introductions were such as to convey no real knowledge of names. Sir Thomas had donned a velvet coat in which he looked both picturesque and imposing.

The meal was entirely vegetarian ; no wine was served, and after dinner nobody smoked. Whatever else Sir Thomas might be, he was obviously an occultist. He was also a man of few words, but when he did speak, it was as one having authority, and all at the table broke off their individual conversations to listen to him.

I forget how the subject of Christian Science cropped up, but I shall never forget him saying : " Christian Science—hmph ! Effective, yes—but only for indolent egos [1] who wish to work off no further bad Karma in present incarnation."

" Very true," said J. M. H.

" One patient miraculously cured of cancer," Sir Thomas pursued, " other patient unmiraculously dies : first patient, spiritual slacker—personality allowed to have its own way ; second patient—personality dominated by ego."

" And that not only applies to diseases," said J. M. H. " How many people long to take up some particular avocation, and find themselves compelled to take up something totally different ! That is the ego's doing, for a

[1] Ego as opposed to personality.

strong ego always aims at progress—hence the line of *most* resistance."

" Ah, indeed," Sir Thomas concurred, " and wise are they who follow the decrees of their own egos, instead of kicking against the pricks. That's where half the world's un-happiness comes in."

I thought of Chris, whose personality must have been so well in line with her ego, that her difficult and restricted life could appear so joyous.

Sir Thomas remained silent for at least five minutes, though he would occasionally smile or nod approval at one remark or another. Yet though he was silent, somehow my eyes kept wandering in his direction, and the more I looked at him, the more remarkable and lovable he appeared. Once more I found myself wondering who and what he was ? Could he possibly be one of the English Masters, and could J. M. H. have been his chela ?

Presently the conversation turned into political channels, and although much of it I could not follow and hence cannot set down in writing, one or two points impressed them-selves on my memory.

"Nations," said J. M. H., "who wouldn't learn through bloodshed are now being forced to learn their mutual interdependence through financial pressure on all sides, which is being manipulated by the Great Ones so that the master-minds of the economic world may realize that Brotherhood is a fact in nature, and *not* a nebulous theory for idealists."

"First principles of Brotherhood preached two thousand years ago by Christ," Sir Thomas contributed, "but ignored because comfortable and inexpensive ; bankruptcy uncomfortable, and in consequence effective." He smiled to himself. "The few learn through philosophy ; the many can only learn through their pockets."

We laughed in appreciation of his caustic and humorous turns of speech.

"Patriotism of the sentimental or Jingo kind," J. M. H. declared, "I mean the 'Rule Britannia' or '*Deutschland über alles*' variety, will have to be sublimated into a genuine desire for international co-operation. Finance must, and eventually *will* be, international. Furthermore, the days of acquiring new colonies are over."

"No more worlds left to conquer," our

host interpolated, " land conquered, sea conquered, air conquered—man reduced to con-
quering invisible worlds, by turning his
consciousness inwards instead of outwards."

" And where will art come in ? " one of the
men asked.

" Only highest forms of art, embodying
great spiritual concepts, will ultimately sur-
vive," Sir Thomas replied. " Art of clever
mediocrities leads but to the dust-bin, because
no great idea behind it. Fed on mannerisms,
it dies of under-nourishment."

We rose from the table and retired to a
lounge-hall where an enormous fire was flam-
ing much too fiercely.

" Tut, tut," said the old gentleman. " Do
my servants want to burn me at the
stake ? "

With remarkable agility for his years, he
fetched a heavy screen from the far corner of
the lounge, and placed it in front of the fire.
I offered my assistance, but he refused it.
He then sat down in an armchair and buried
himself in a large leather-backed tome. Two
of the young men played chess, while the third
looked on. Our hostess played patience, and
J. M. H. and myself were left to talk. After

a while he proposed we should take a turn outside. We paced up and down the terrace in the moonlight.

" What a lovable old gentleman," was my first remark. " But it's a bit curious to be accepting hospitality without having heard the name of one's host."

" He who is asked questions and does not *know* is exempted from telling lies," was the answer. After that I asked no more questions on the subject.

" Lyall Herbert is coming to-morrow," he vouchsafed after a pause.

I was genuinely pleased and said so. It did not seem quite fair that I should be the only one to know of J. M. H.'s return.

" And Toni Bland ? " I asked. " I suppose you know what a bad time he's going through ? "

" I do."

" You'll see him, of course ? "

" No," he said.

I was taken aback. " But think what it would mean to him to see you ! " I couldn't help saying.

He smiled a little sadly. " Even compassion must be tempered with wisdom.

Were I to help Toni Bland now, I should
retard his progress for years to come."

" That seems very strange."

" The workings of Karma are always
strange. But what a man's ego decrees may
not be altered, even by his Guru. As there
are foolish ' climbers ' in the world of snobbery,
so, as opposed to Sir Thomas's ' spiritual
slackers,' there are ' spiritual climbers ' in the
world of occultism—Toni is one of the latter,
and he must climb *alone.*"

" But at least you could give him some
comfort." . . .

" Does the physician administer a narcotic
to dull pain when he knows it can only retard
progress ? " He paused for a moment and
then added : " There are some we can help
the more by not helping them at all. Comfort
is only a subtle form of temporary help."

" And my wife ? " I asked.

" She too is a ' climber,' and because of that
she is a sick woman. Doctors may aid her
a little, but the day of her cure is not yet.
She will progress through suffering and you
will progress through patience. In a previous
life she tended you ; in this life you shall tend
her. And do it well, my son."

" What I meant was whether you intend to see her ? "

He shook his head. " I would only make matters worse if I did."

" I really can't understand that," I exclaimed, knowing how disappointed Viola would be.

" If you understood everything, you'd have no more to learn. And yet—if you particularly wish to know, you may ask your friend."

" Anrias, you mean ? "

" I do."

" You consider he's reliable ? " I asked. " I don't mean his astrology, I mean his power to ' tune-in ' to the Masters. One has to be so careful."

" Clairvoyants who can merely *see* are apt to be deluded," he answered, " but he who can discriminate between one set of vibrations and another may be relied upon. Yes, you can trust your friend."

We left the terrace and walked along a labyrinth of paths, across which the trees cast strange shadows in the moonlight. There were still many questions I should have liked to ask, but I sensed that J. M. H. was in a meditative mood and so did not wish to break in on his reflections. The air had grown chilly and I shivered. " We will go back into the house," he said at length.

The two men had just finished their game of chess as we entered, and Sir Thomas was standing over them, pointing to the board.

" Troublesome fellow, that knight," he said. " Queen should have disposed of him five moves ago."

" But his castle was in the way," objected the loser.

" Tut, tut, you should have taken that two moves previously with pawn. Good night," he said abruptly, waving his hand to us all ; then he disappeared.

QUESTION : You say that while Truth may be approached solely by individual effort, work on the other hand must be collective and organized by authority. The Occult Brotherhood of Adepts is a group of men who, like yourself, have liberated themselves from all limitations and have attained to Truth ; but like yourself, have undertaken certain self-chosen work in advancing the general welfare of the world. They inspire great reforms in every department of life and work by methods of which very little is known, but which are immensely effective. Their co-operation is complete, their organization perfect, they recognize an absolute ruler—but in life they are entirely free. Such a mode of living seems to be the logical outcome of your teaching. Do you deny that this is so ? Or does your challenge apply rather to the popular confusion of Truth with organized work for the service of humanity ?

KRISHNAMURTI : First of all you must understand what I mean by collective and organized work. You state that there is an occult brotherhood which organizes work for humanity for advancing the welfare of the world. To assume that there are those who have knowledge, who have realized Truth, and because of that realization use methods of which, as is said, very little is known, choosing special agents and messengers to do their work and inspiring worthy organizations—to me this assumption is based upon an illusion, leading to exploitation of man for his " good." . . .

—" *Star Bulletin*," *September*, 1931.

CHAPTER XI

THE TRUTH ABOUT KRISHNAMURTI

A CONCERT of innumerable birds woke me up next morning, and I looked out of my window on to a blaze of daffodils, sparkling with dewdrops in the sun. But if I was an early riser, Sir Thomas had outdone me, for I caught sight of him, in his skull-cap as usual, wandering down one of the paths which skirted a large flower-bed. Occasionally he would bend down to examine one or other of the plants, or to caress a big dog which sedately walked beside him. Presently he was joined by his niece, who gave him a kiss, in response to which he affectionately patted her cheek ; then they strolled down the path together, round a bend and out of sight.

There was still an hour and a half till breakfast, so I dressed leisurely, and, following my host's example, wandered forth into the garden. I felt so drawn to the old gentleman that I hoped I should meet him. At the same time, I was chary of intruding on his privacy. But in any case I was to be disappointed, for I did not see him again till lunch-time.

That lunch was a memorable occasion. There were only four of us present—Sir Thomas, J. M. H., myself and one of the other men. The latter was a few minutes late, and came in when the rest of us were already seated. In his hand was Krishnamurti's *Star Bulletin*. He opened it, then handed it to Sir Thomas, indicating a certain passage. The old gentleman read it, vouchsafed no comment, beyond his usual non-committal " Tut, tut . . ." and passed it on to J. M. H., who glanced at it, smiled significantly at Sir Thomas, then put it aside. But I was not going to let such an opportunity slip. At last I might be in the position to hear something really authoritative on the vexed question of Krishnamurti.

" The *Star Bulletin*. . . . I take it myself. But as you see," I added, smiling, " I still believe in Masters."

" I'm glad somebody does," Sir Thomas remarked with good-natured irony ; " dear, dear, if Krishnamurti's ideas were universally accepted, some of us might as well take our departure to other planets."

I instantly pricked up my ears and glanced at J. M. H., who only said in an undertone : " Many a true word——" leaving me mentally to complete the saying.

" Then I take it, Sir Thomas," I ventured to ask, " you don't altogether approve of Krishnamurti's methods ? "

" Unfortunately he *has* no proper methods since he took the Arhat initiation, and ceased to be the medium for the Lord Maitreya.[1] Better if he had retired from public life to meditate in seclusion, as Arhats did in bygone days."

" I'm a bit hazy about that Arhat initiation," I whispered to the man beside me.

" It's the one in which the Master withdraws all guidance from His pupil, who may have to negotiate the most difficult problems without being allowed to ask any questions," he

[1] The Lord Maitreya is He who, every two thousand years, fulfils His office of World-Teacher by overshadowing a specially prepared medium, in order to give forth a new Teaching suitable for the future development of mankind. The last time, two thousand years ago, Jesus became His medium and yielded himself up for the purpose at the age of thirty.   A similar destiny was anticipated for Krishnamurti.

explained ; " he has to rely entirely on his own judgment, and if he makes mistakes, must bear the consequences."

" And so what did Krishnamurti do ? " my host interpolated, obviously having heard. " Like the proverbial manservant who knows he's about to be given notice, *he* gave notice first. In other words, he cut himself adrift from the White Lodge, and repudiated all of us."

" And unfortunately," J. M. H. added, " he induced others far below him in spiritual evolution to do likewise. Also instead of giving forth the new Teaching so badly needed, he escaped from the responsibilities of his office as prophet and teacher by reverting to a past incarnation, and an ancient philosophy of his own race with which you are familiar, but which is useless for the Western World in the present Cycle."

" Then we were right ! " I exclaimed. " It *is* Advaita he's teaching ? "

He nodded.

" But those to whom he speaks think they are receiving a new message, and as such it carries undue weight," Sir Thomas contributed. " The message he should have delivered, he has failed to deliver—or only partly delivered. Nothing about Art—no plans for the new sub-race—educational schemes dropped—and in place of all this : Advaita, a philosophy for chelas, and one of the most easily misunderstood paths to Liberation."

" Then are we to assume," I hazarded, " that Krishnamurti's mission has been a complete failure ? "

" Friend," said the old gentleman, " you ask many questions ; to what use will you put the answers if we give them to you ? "

It was on the tip of my tongue to apologize, but instead I felt impelled to speak what was in my mind. " Sir Thomas," I replied, " because of Krishnamurti, many people are in great distress ; if you'll be gracious enough to enlighten me a little, perhaps I may be able to enlighten *them*."

" Good ! " he exclaimed, " the motive is pure ; your questions shall be answered."

I began to express my gratitude, but he waved it aside with a kindly gesture, and proceeded : " He who attempts to teach Advaita, and omits all Sanscrit terms, courts failure. Sanscrit words engender an occult vibration which is lost when translated. Western words not suitable to describe subjective states of consciousness, because their associations are mainly mundane." He paused a moment to continue his lunch, then added : " Well did my Brother Koot Hoomi say that Krishnamurti had destroyed all the many stairways to God, while his own remains incomplete."

" And would never be suitable for *all* types, in any case," J. M. H. put in.

" Also, being incomplete," the old gentleman took up the thread again, " it may lead to dangers unforeseen by those who attempt to climb it. Danger Number One : Krishnamurti's casting aside of time-honoured definitions and classifications leaves aspirant without true scale of values. Danger Number Two : climbing his particular stairway necessitates constant meditation, which in its turn necessitates constant protection from Guru—and Guru not allowed by Krishnamurti," he concluded with a twinkle.

" But," I asked, " is the Guru's protection *always* necessary for meditation—I mean even when it's done in small doses ? "

" Of course, a moderate degree may be practised in safety without a Guru," J. M. H.

replied, " but as Sir Thomas says, long-continued meditation leads to states of consciousness and excursions on to other planes where the Master's guidance is absolutely indispensable. Another flaw in this pseudo-Advaita which Krishnamurti is giving out, is that he addresses the personality, the physical-plane man, as if he were the Monad or at least the Ego. Of course the Monad, the Divine Spark, is the Absolute Existence-Knowledge-Bliss, and hence eternally free, but that doesn't mean that the personality down here, immersed in endless-seeming Karmic difficulties, can share its consciousness, or even that of the Ego—the link between the personality and the Monad. Krishnamurti's Advaitism, which is not to be confounded with the recognized form of that noble philosophy, will, I fear, lead his followers nowhere except perhaps to hypocrisy and self-delusion."

Sir Thomas nodded assent. " And while he has directed them to repudiate all Masters, he refuses to act as Guru to them himself." The old gentleman was silent for a moment, then shook his head mournfully. " Children crying in the night of spiritual darkness, and no one to comfort them. . . . He who could help, won't, and we who might help, can't, for Doubt has poisoned their belief in our very existence. No wonder Koot Hoomi's face looks a little sad." He turned to the large dog which, all this while, with remarkable canine self-control, had sat perfectly still, gazing up at him ; and as he patted him, he said : " My friend, if even the King told you your master was superfluous, I don't think you'd believe him, eh ? "

The dog wagged his tail, and touchingly snuggled up against Sir Thomas's knee.

It was a picture I shall not forget : the oak-panelled room, the old pictures, the long refectory table, the sun pouring in through the diamond-paned windows, and finally that impressive and lovable old gentleman in his velvet skull-cap, with his faithful companion by his side. I was transported back to a world in which hooting motor-cars, turmoil and rush seemed but the jarring trivialities of a nightmare.

And yet amidst this atmosphere of old-world serenity, unseen powers were at work, controlling and directing the schemes of mankind. How honoured I felt that Sir Thomas had trusted me sufficiently no longer to conceal the fact that he was a Master.

The manservant had entered to bring the next course, and had withdrawn again. I noticed that he never appeared unless summoned by means of the electric bell-button within reach of Sir Thomas's hand. Evidently conversation, even at meals, was frequently of a nature too important to be overheard.

I had still some questions to ask about Krishnamurti, but was momentarily at a loss how to frame them, without seeming indiscreet.

" You'll forgive me," I said to my host, " if I go back to the subject we were discussing."

" What! More questions? " he replied with mock severity, " you'll be presenting us with a questionnaire next ; well, what are they ? "

" You'll perhaps remember I asked you if Krishnamurti's mission must be regarded as a total failure."

" True, true. A success while still overshadowed by the World-Teacher, as I implied before—a failure afterwards. He did good work in teaching people to use their own brains, and in showing them . . ." He broke off and waved his hand towards J. M. H. " Come, come," he said with a twinkle, " this is your chela and you leave the old gentleman to do all the work ! "

" He is in better hands than mine," said J. M. H., laughing. Nevertheless he continued : " Krishnamurti came to break up the old order of things in preparation for the new, but he broke up too much of the past and prepared nothing for the future. Yet the old order is finished and may not be revived. The day of blind obedience to leaders is over—salvation cannot be reached merely by worshipping personalities and accepting as gospel everything they say, for to accept is not of necessity to understand. Even so exalted a Being as the Lord Buddha said : ' Do not believe everything merely because I say it.' "

" He may be termed a forerunner, needed in this particular Cycle, but not actually the World-Teacher," Sir Thomas put in ; " World-Teacher not expected by us till end of century."

" Yet why should even a forerunner——" I began.

" Who shall judge another without know-ing his difficulties ? " Sir Thomas cut me short. " A quality has its defects. Need I ask you if you've ever heard *Parsifal* ? No, for you love music, as I do. Krishnamurti is endowed with Parsifal-like simplicity. Because he has reached a certain state of consciousness and evolution, in his modesty he fails to see that others have *not* reached it likewise. There-fore he prescribes for others what is only suitable for himself."

He rose from his high-backed chair. " Come," he said to the dog, " we will take a stroll in the garden and pay our respects to the daffodils before my visitor arrives. At four in the library," he added to J. M. H., and went out.

CHAPTER XII

AFTER lunch J. M. H. took me to the lily-pond, a secluded spot in the garden surrounded by evergreens. It was beautiful to the ear as well as to the eye, for a small cascade made exquisite music as it trickled among mossy boulders. Facing the pond was a stone seat, and on this we sat down and contemplated the large flat leaves of the water-lilies, above which a pair of early yellow butterflies chased each other in the sunlight. There was an atmosphere of celestial peace over the whole scene, and J. M. H. told me that Sir Thomas frequently came there to meditate.

We had been silent for a long time, and J. M. H. seemed far away in thought, then suddenly he made a gesture as if to bring himself back to the material world.

"Remember well all you heard at lunch," he said, "it is more important even

144

than you realize. Later on you will know why."

I assured him I was not in the least likely to forget.

" Very good," he said, " and now ask me anything that is on your mind. Time is none too plentiful."

I longed to ask him many things about himself, but refrained, for such questions would have savoured too much of personal curiosity, and I felt prompted to confine myself to such matters of importance as bore relation to immediate problems. All that I had just heard had enlightened me considerably, yet on several points I was still puzzled.

" Well," he said, regarding me with a smile, " are the questions so difficult ? "

" To put them concisely—yes. However . . . Last century the Masters gave out certain teachings to help on evolution through Their medium, H. P. B., didn't They ? "

" True."

" They used her and the Theosophical Society to make humanity realize Their existence——"

" Quite so."

" Well now, apparently They've set up

another medium who's calmly repudiated the
T.S. and the Masters Themselves, and who,
if you please, ungratefully refers to all
mediumship and overshadowing as exploitation : what does it mean ? "

" It means that the Masters are neither
omnipotent nor omniscient," J. M. H. replied.
" They have to be content with the best
instrument They can find at the moment for
Their purpose, but They cannot be certain
in advance how the experiment will work.
However pure the medium may be, he may still
have to contend with all sorts of external difficulties which could not have been anticipated.
If he is young and handsome, he may, for
instance, be swamped by the adoration and
adulation of women, their jealousies and so
forth; and the more sensitive he is, the more
disorganizing all this may prove." He paused
for a moment, and then said gravely : " The
expression of love demands almost more
wisdom than anything else. To know how,
when and where to love needs the utmost
discrimination. If Krishnamurti has not
achieved all that was hoped, the fault does
not lie entirely with him. . . . As a matter
of fact," he pursued with an altered inflection,

" not men, but women make the best mediums
for the Great Ones. That is why H. P. B.
and A. B. took female bodies. Men are better
constituted to be occultists, women to be
mediums. A woman, by her very nature,
yields herself, or rather her higher vehicles,
more readily to the Master than does a man."
He picked up a leaf from the ground and idly
toyed with it. " Altogether mediumship of
this very exalted type is a highly delicate and
complicated matter. Only those who have
worked out all their personal desires and
repressions can really become *willing* mediums
for the Masters—and these experience ecstasy,
as did your friend who passed over . . . The
unwilling ones feel they are being exploited
and experience a sense of frustration. Krishnamurti from the start was an unwilling
medium, and only because the world was in
such a serious condition did the Lord Maitreya
risk the experiment of overshadowing him."
He bent down to caress a robin which had
been fearlessly hopping about near his feet.
The little bird perched on his finger for a few
moments, fluttered its wings happily, then
flew away. I was about to comment on this
charming picture, when J. M. H. turned to

me and continued : " It cannot be sufficiently
stressed that the Higher Ones are limited in
the expression of Their power on the physical
plane ; limited by the personal karma of the
individuals They may wish to help, and which
even They are not permitted to set aside ;
and finally, and perhaps most seriously limited
by this ever-increasing wave of Doubt,
destroying those very connecting-links through
which alone help may be given from the
higher to the lower planes. It is not too
much to say that every soul who loses faith
in the Masters, weakens the expression of
Their force down here. Some have lost faith
because they imagined the Great Ones have
an entirely free hand to carry out Their
schemes for the welfare of Their chelas or
humanity at large, and have wavered in their
allegiance as soon as these schemes have
failed to materialize. Others again, confused
and bewildered in their minds, have come
more and more to accept the idea that Those
to whom they once looked for help and guidance are purely mythical figures. Thus some
doubt the Masters' existence because they see
no evidence of Their power, and others doubt
because their whole outlook has been dis-

torted. Yet both those whose belief has been shaken by what would appear to be Their failures, and those for whom it has been shattered by baffling doctrines, may be assured that despite the darkness of the times, despite the limitations placed upon the Masters Themselves in the outside world, Their Love and Compassion are never-failing . . . and though They may not work miracles to lift the burden from the suffering and the weary, They are glad and ready to give of Their spiritual strength to those who still have the faith to ask for it. . . ."

There was a long silence, broken only by an early songful thrush perched in a neighbouring tree.

I reflected upon what he had said, but in the end was constrained to ask what the upshot of it all would be. " You see," I pointed out, " the difficulty of trying to combat this doubt and misery that's been stirred up, is that people imagine they dare not criticize someone they think to be the World-Teacher——"

" And yet who *now* teaches them that nobody, however exalted, can teach them anything at all," J. M. H. completed.

" But those were almost the very words Toni Bland used ! " I exclaimed in surprise.

" And I impressed him to use them," he returned quietly.

" You—you can impress Toni like that ? "

" Why not ? " J. M. H. smiled. " I have been training him for years to be receptive to my thoughts."

" That accounts for it, then. . . . He used to come out with the most enlightening things. And Viola was so drawn to him, too. . . ." I was certainly astounded at this discovery. Not a word had Toni ever mentioned on the subject. My thoughts reverted to that day when he had first come to tea with us. " But why should you have troubled to impress him just on that occasion ? " I couldn't help asking ; " there was only Mrs. Saxton and——"

He stopped me. " Has Mrs. Saxton derived either happiness or spiritual benefit from her repudiation of the Masters ? "

" I should hardly think so," I laughed.

" Many years ago, you took me to see her : why'? "

" Oh . . . well, I thought you might be able to help her a bit. But I'm afraid she's a hopeless case."

" If you saw a blind dog, however unattractive and insignificant, heading for a precipice, would you not try to stop it ? "

" Certainly ! "

" Well, I merely tried to stop that woman from falling over . . . though without much hope of success," he added.

Suddenly another woman whom J. M. H. had helped came into my mind. " By the way," I said, " that last book I wrote about you——"

He nodded interrogatively.

" Your remarks on jealousy, or rather non-jealousy—I'm afraid some people have misunderstood them a bit."

" People misunderstand many things when it suits their purpose."

" You remember Gertrude Wilton ? "

" I do. She sometimes honours me by sending a thought in my direction," he smiled.

" Then you know what I'm going to say ? "

" Words have been given us to exchange ideas with," he rejoined, " why not use them ? What about Gertrude Wilton ? "

" She's appointed herself a Pioneer of the New Morality, and her husband doesn't like it. *I* was drawn into the matter."

J. M. H. looked somewhat amused. " As arbiter ? " he queried.

" More or less. *He* even wanted me to write to you about it. So did others in the same sort of dilemma."

" So I have brought dishonour to husbands ? " he said, but his eyes were smiling.

" To do this one justice, that wasn't the side of it that rankled. As a matter of fact, he behaved very decently. . . ."

" True," J. M. H. interpolated, " he has acquired merit."

" But when it came to his wife's blazoning it all over the place and pretending the whole affair was—well—merely to elevate her lover's soul . . ."

" And what steps did you take ? " J. M. H. asked.

" I told her if she *must* have this affair, she must also face the fact that she was having it for her own pleasure, and cut out the advance-guard-of-morality business."

J. M. H. laughed.

" I also recommended her at least to consider her husband's position, and not proclaim it from the house-tops. Was I right ? "

" There was nothing else you could have

done in the circumstances. And I think it has had the desired effect," he added after a few moments in which he appeared to be sensing up what had actually happened. Then he said : " There is no one so dishonest with herself as a woman who wishes to go along the path of her own inclinations."

" That's what I told her."

" Good," he applauded. " You have evidently learnt something about women in your present incarnation—which is more than a great many men can say ! " He proceeded to tell me how the Masters try to adjust the balance of morals, and why at one time he had put forward his ideas about non-jealousy.[1]

" Jealousy with men," he explained, " began as an instinct to protect the fœtus. If a pregnant woman indulges in promiscuity, she injures the unborn child by becoming the recipient of mixed magnetism. Jealousy in its original form was therefore a protection against this contingency, but like many legitimate instincts, it got out of hand and degenerated into an excuse for possessiveness, cruelty and kindred evils, including murder and suicide. Through jealousy thou-

[1] See *The Initiate in the New World*, Chapter XIV.

sands of homes were broken up and children were deprived of the benefits of family life. To counteract all this it was necessary to put forward the ideal of non-jealousy, which in its day was startling and in advance of the times. Yet as all ideals can be distorted and used for selfish purposes, so has this one also been distorted. The teachings on the subject I gave out some years ago are still applicable to Latin races and to such individuals who are consumed by jealous passions, but for the more enlightened types they are already *vieux jeu*. In any case the relations between the sexes are in a stage of transition, which will require on both sides adjustments of a very subtle nature." He outlined for me the characteristics we may expect to see in both the men and the women of the comparatively near future, and how these characteristics will react on morals ; but what he told me may not yet be given out to the world.

He got up from the seat. " I must now leave you," he said ; " I shall be engaged until dinner-time."

CHAPTER XIII

THE FUTURE OF THE BRITISH RACE

Lyall Herbert had arrived and had spent an hour in private with J. M. H. before the evening meal. I was afterwards permitted to know that part of the interview had been devoted to a dissertation on the esoteric aspects of music. Herbert had already written a book on the subject, but further information was to be disseminated through the medium of articles or possibly through another book.

I looked forward to meals at Sir Thomas's with especial pleasure ; for one thing my host was present, and for another they afforded me an opportunity for acquiring knowledge not to be gleaned elsewhere.

That evening a variety of subjects, all having an occult significance, were discoursed upon ; but I have since been requested to use my discretion as to how much may be revealed in these pages.

Sir Thomas made a most interesting prognostication to the effect that in the coming age all the arts would be more scientific in character, that is to say specific artistic effects, whether of colour, sound, form or rhythm, would be consciously and deliberately used to produce specific results. For one thing, in place of the ultra-modern music which has proved so ear-splitting to the uninitiated, and was solely put through to break up old conventions and baneful thought-forms, musicians will be inspired by the Devas to bring down combinations of sounds from the Higher Planes to help and to heal. "Music to become more purposeful," he explained in his terse manner, " even religion to become more scientific. The rôle of priests partly to be allocated to musicians, partly to trained psycho-analysts. Effects of music in time will replace effects of ceremonial ; psycho-analysis will replace confessional-box. Too much loftiness of character expected of priests —result, disappointment. Not so much expected of artists."

He lapsed into silence, but J. M. H. elaborated a few points relative to psycho-analysis and some of the immediate difficulties connected with it. " Of course," he said, " the ideal would be if it could be mainly practised by advanced occultists, instead of the materialists of the present day, some of whom risk delving so deep into the subconscious, that they uncover memories of past incarnations without even realizing what they are doing. The occultist, with clairvoyant vision, could tell from the reactions on his patient's subtler bodies at what point to stop in the analysis : that point being usually within the time-limit of the present life. But the materialist, scoffing, perhaps, at the idea of past lives and therefore fumbling in the dark, may churn up memories far more remote, which fill the mind of a sensitive patient with horror. The disclosure of all these lusts and passions, experienced in bygone ages and under different moral codes—all the forgotten dregs of previous lives, in fact, yet not recognized as such either by him or the practitioner—may lead to dangerous states of self-abasement and melancholia."

" The Lords of Karma have closed the door of memory for a purpose," Sir Thomas said gravely. " It is not well that a man's consciousness be burdened with knowledge of the past before he has the strength to bear it. Psycho-analysis not a toy for children. Like fire—either destructive or purifying. Therefore, as J. M. H. says, only seers and occultists can direct it wisely."

He paused for a while, and a curiously impressive silence filled the room. Then at last he spoke again. " I gather from Him before Whom the future lies like an open book, that even the materialistic analysts of times to come will be forced to realize that analysis of the subconscious mind is useless unless the patient's Ego is powerful enough not only to make the personality face the process of disintegration with sanity, but afterwards to build up, and take over the full control of that subconscious mind itself."

Another subject discoursed upon was the future of the British people. Sir Thomas reminded us that sooner or later every race enters upon a critical stage of its history. During the next three hundred years our own race would be confronted with a choice.

" Romans incarnating less," he maintained, " their imperialistic work done. More Greeks incarnating instead. Hence a new type of man appearing. Greek capacity for meta-

physical thought manifesting as new form
of idealism and potentiality to turn inwards
and contact higher worlds ; Greek love of
beauty manifesting as artistic feeling.   Draw-
back of the former—increasing disability to
deal with problems of physical plane.   Draw-
back of latter—the old Greek leaning towards
homosexuality.   How to deal with it—that is
our problem.   A new teaching will have to be
evolved.   If those homosexual tendencies are
allowed to run riot, Britain is doomed after
the manner of ancient Greece ; but if they
are sublimated through the metaphysical
element, she will ascend to heights of spiritual
and artistic glory, and become the Pioneer
Race along that line.   The choice is at hand "
—he drummed his fingers on the table to
emphasize his point—" spiritual idealism or
descent into the racial abyss ! "

There was a pause, then J. M. H. said :
" Homosexuality in Greece was partly the
result of the perversion of certain teachings
put forward by some Adepts of the Platonic
School.   The average woman in Greece was
not expected to be intellectual, therefore man
was dependent on his own sex for the exchange
of metaphysical ideas.   To further this mental

interchange, these Adepts endeavoured to inspire that idealistic and self-sacrificing friendship between men which has so often been portrayed in Greek literature. That it should have degenerated into the grosser forms of homosexuality was a blot on the moral escutcheon of the race, which They had neither intended nor anticipated."

" You have mentioned the women of Greece, but what about the women of to-day and of the future ? " I ventured to ask.

" Because men are turning inwards," J. M. H. replied, " women are turning outwards."

" Balance must be adjusted somehow," Sir Thomas interpolated.

" Quite so," J. M. H. assented. " As the new type of man is to be more retiring and introspective, as Sir Thomas implies, the women, on the other hand, will become greater organizers, more competent in business, and so forth."

" Plenty of brains, but likely to lose their intuition," our host added. " Inferior example of new type of woman in danger of developing pronounced power-complex ; inferior example of new type of

man in danger of becoming a drone, owing
to constitutional dreaminess and consequent
inefficiency in mundane matters. It is well
my niece is not present," he concluded,
" very feminine woman—prospect not invit-
ing—men to be women, women to be men
—dear, dear, dear . . ." He rose from the
table amid the laughter which his remark
and manner of making it had called forth.

After dinner Lyall Herbert played to us,
and it was obvious that Sir Thomas possessed
a marked appreciation of music. He listened
intently with closed eyes, from time to time
waving his hand in accordance with the
rhythm, as a particular phrase or melody
especially appealed to him.

When Lyall had finished, he nodded to
him with evident pleasure.

" You have many difficulties in your musical
life," he assumed rather than asked. " Those
who work for the Masters find obstacles
strewn on the path of recognition."

Herbert's face lighted up ; he too had
obviously fallen under the spell of our host.
" I certainly do have difficulties," he agreed.

"Hm—perhaps if some big-wig in the
Theosophical world *before* the era of Krishna-

murti had labelled you an initiate," Sir
Thomas observed dryly, " a band of enthusi-
asts would have rallied round you and pushed
you into the limelight—eh ? "

" But I'm afraid I'm not an initiate," Lyall
smiled.

" Maybe not." He shook his head reflec-
tively. " In any case I never did approve
of all that labelling. Initiates here, initiates
there. Medals and decorations, rewards in
heaven, tut, tut . . . Initiation a private
and sacred matter between Masters and pupils
—inexpedient to make it public—exceptions
of course——" He smiled and left us.

" You little know how much honoured
you've been," said J. M. H. to Herbert.

" Are you quite sure I don't ? " Herbert
replied.

J. M. H. smiled and said nothing.

It was arranged that Herbert and I should
travel back to London together the following
afternoon. But we spent half an hour with
J. M. H. before our departure. We were both
completely in the dark as to his policy or
intended movements. Were we allowed to
write and tell Arkwright of his return, for
instance ? This thought came into my head

as the three of us were strolling up and down the lawn before lunch. He obviously read my thoughts, for he said : " You have seen Arkwright ? "

" He visited us in London," I replied.

" You may write and tell him the missing Guru has been found," he rejoined, " that is —if you wish ! "

" And is he to tell the others in America ? " I asked.

" I have written to Heddon, who will have already told them what is necessary."

I felt a sense of relief. I had been truly sorry for all those chelas in Boston ; now, whatever he might have directed Heddon to tell them, they would at least know he was still alive.

J. M. H. also gave me a message for Toni Bland, but I was to use my own discretion as to the moment when it should be delivered. More than this cryptic injunction he did not vouchsafe on the subject. He then adjured us to preserve the utmost secrecy with regard to our stay at Sir Thomas's house and all we had experienced there, though he allowed me to make an exception in favour of my wife. " Tell her that the period of darkness for her is nearing its end, and that soon she will be able to *see* once more, but with an enhanced vision which will compensate her for all the suffering that Karma has imposed upon her. Some acquire balance through mental suffering, some through physical ; she has acquired it through both, and because of this, her powers will be the more reliable when they return."

I was deeply grateful for this message, for I knew what it would mean to Viola, and that in some measure it would console her for not having been with us.

But J. M. H. had yet one thing more to say : within a time not specified, he would send for us again, and for a purpose to be revealed later. And he intimated that this second visit would mark a very important step in our evolution.

We were to leave for London immediately after lunch.

The big blue car was at the door. With regret I bade J. M. H. good-bye, then turned to Sir Thomas to express my thanks for all that I had received at his hands.

" Waste no words on gratitude." He made a good-humoured gesture of distaste. " Can

I not read the heart ? " He held my hand
for a moment, and added : " I give you an
old man's blessing."

" And I accept it as a Master's . . ." I
replied reverently, but so low as not to be
overheard.

" Tut, tut . . ." he reproved me, yet he
was human enough, I could see, not to be
really displeased, which made him the more
endearing. He said good-bye to Herbert, to
whom he also gave his blessing, and then we
got into the car. I can still see the picture
of him and J. M. H. standing on the topmost
of the massive stone steps leading to the front
door, with the large dog seated sedately
between them, as they watched us drive off.

Sir Thomas's chauffeur was an astonish-
ingly swift driver, and even if I had wanted
to read the signposts on the road, I could
hardly have done so, as we whizzed past them
at such a rate.

Herbert and I had a carriage to ourselves
the greater part of the journey to London.
Did he realize that Sir Thomas was a Master,
I wondered ?

" A remarkable old gentleman," I remarked
cautiously, with a view to finding out.

His expression gave me the information I desired.

We were naturally eager to know what was in store for us on that next occasion when we should again be allowed to visit Sir Thomas, and speculated at length on the subject.

" Occultism's so marvellously full of surprises and romance," Lyall observed, " how dull ordinary life must seem without it."

" What—even to composers ? " I queried.

" Composing without any ideal behind it— what is it ? " He shrugged. " Art for Art's sake is all very well as a high-sounding catchphrase, but Art for the Masters' and Humanity's sake is much more romantic."

I heartily agreed with him.

CHAPTER XIV

A SOUL IN DARKNESS

I HAD plenty to tell Viola when I got home, and of course she was greatly cheered by J. M. H.'s message, though at the same time disappointed that she was not allowed to see him. I told her the curious reason he gave— namely, that for her to see him now would do her harm rather than good—but that only served to rouse her curiosity.

" Well, you must ask David about it," I said at last. " J. M. H. told me *he* would know."

" A lot of good that is ! " she replied, " when he's gone away and left us, the dirty dog. . . ."

" Then you'll just have to possess your soul in patience," I laughed.

" Oh, by the way," she said, changing the subject, " Miss Hart called."

" Oh——? "

" Mrs. Saxton's lying dangerously ill in a

nursing home. She was persuaded into having an operation for something or other, and now she's not expected to live."

" Poor thing ! "

" Miss Hart rang up to know how she was and they told her the operation had been a great success . . ."

" But that she was dying, eh ? " I completed. " Usual thing, surgeons perfectly satisfied, *but* . . ."

" It's all rather sad," Viola went on, " both her daughters in India and she's got nobody else in the world—and a nursing home of all places to die in. . . . Can you imagine anything more dreary ? "

A few days later I received a telephone call from the Matron of the nursing home, thanking me for some flowers we had sent, and saying that Mrs. Saxton was particularly anxious for me to go and see her. I agreed, of course, to do so, especially in view of what J. M. H. had told me. Now I was perhaps to understand what he had meant by his allusion to the blind dog and the precipice.

When I arrived at the home, a dragon in uniform gave me the usual injunctions to make my visit as brief as possible, so as not to tire the patient. She even implied that Mrs. Saxton was being very wilful in desiring to see me at all. These unflattering aspersions, however, left me cold—though to placate the dragon I favoured her with one of my most studied smiles and promised all that was required of me.

I found Mrs. Saxton in a pitiable condition, so changed, in fact, as to be hardly recognizable. The nurse lingered in the room until requested to go, and even then threatened to come and turn me out if I overstepped the time-limit.

" I can't even die in peace," Mrs. Saxton muttered fretfully, " without those nurses trying to interfere with me."

I expressed my sympathy. There was a pause in which she seemed to be searching for words.

" I'm all alone," she said at last.

" But isn't there any friend you'd like to see ? " I asked.

" Only one—Christabel—and she's dead . . ." Her hands moved restlessly upon the sheet. Then with an effort : " *You* believe there's . . . something—afterwards, don't you ? "

"Most certainly I do."

"*He* says *now* it's . . . it's all illusion. . . ." I could only assume that she alluded to Krishnamurti and his teachings. "And when I wanted him to explain . . . he wouldn't see me."

"Oh, not illusion in the sense *you* think," I protested, "you've misunderstood him. And I'm sure he'd have seen you if he'd been able to."

"He's taken everything from me," she continued with difficulty, ignoring my reassurance, "everything I used to believe in . . . and now——" Tears were in her frightened eyes.

Again I tried to assure her she had misunderstood, but she did not seem to hear me. She could only follow her own train of thought and repeat disjointedly : "I wanted him to explain—did so want him to *explain*—and he wouldn't see me. . . ."

There was another long pause, and I was completely at a loss how to comfort her.

"That book you wrote about a Master——" she began once more, after a struggle to control the physical pain she was suffering.

" Yes ? " I said eagerly.

" He wasn't like that. . . . He was always willing to help."

" Masters are always willing to help," I murmured, bending over her, for I could see her strength was failing.

" But—but are you sure . . . They——"

" Am I sure They exist ? " I completed the pitiful broken sentence. " I'm as sure as that I exist myself."

" Then why did . . . *he* say . . . They don't ? " Her brow was wrinkled in a tortured frown.

" He didn't—he didn't. . . ." But how could I argue with a dying woman whose reasoning-powers—the few she ever possessed —were failing fast ? She was yearning once again to believe in the Masters, but what means could I adopt to convince her ? She was frightened to die, and perhaps, with the remnants of her pride, reluctant to admit it. If anyone was in need of a Master's comfort, it was she.

Suddenly I resolved to send a powerful thought for help to J. M. H.

Mrs. Saxton had been breathing with diffi-culty, but she was quieter now.

" Tell me what troubles you most ? " I asked gently.

" All alone . . ." she repeated. " So lonely . . . *dark* . . . If only—your Master——"
The last word was a mere gasp, and I was on the point of summoning the nurse, when I noticed that her expression had changed and that she appeared to be seeing something I myself could not see.

" Golden light everywhere . . ." she murmured, " lovely . . ."

But she was seeing no earthly light on that dull London day with the rain beating against the windows of that comfortless room. She had evidently become clairvoyant as many dying people do. From her disjointed muttered phrases I realized with gratitude that a Master must have appeared to her, and she had seen the radiance of His aura of love.

Yet it was not my Guru, but I think Master K. H. who came to her in His deep compassion for all who suffer. . . .

I believe Chris must have been with Him too, for the dying woman murmured her name as if she were present. That terrified expression, so pitiful to see, had gone, and a look of serenity and content had come over her face. Even her physical pain had left her, for her restless hands were still at last.

The nurse came back into the room to reproach me for staying so long, but the patient had fallen asleep.

As I walked home in the rain, I understood. J. M. H. had foreseen everything. He knew that the philosophy Mrs. Saxton had embraced and so lamentably failed to understand or to live up to would prove as comfortless to her in the end as a stone to a starving man. By impressing Toni in the manner he admitted having done that day at our house, he had endeavoured at least to throw out a warning and give her food for thought. But she had disregarded that warning, and the state of despair in which I found her was the result.

At any rate in the end, Mrs. Saxton died peacefully in her sleep soon after I left.

*　　*　　*　　*　　*

Toni's ordeal was over at last. The long-protracted trial had come to an end, and although he was exonerated from all blame, he was left with a considerably reduced income and a difficult time was doubtless in store for him. In view of all this, I was anxious to see him and express the sympathy I felt. He came round for a meal in response to my telephone call, and his altered appearance showed all too clearly how much he had gone through. He remarked plaintively that some people were giving him the cold shoulder, just because he had been involved in this disastrous affair, and had figured in the law-courts.

" Even though I've been proved innocent of all criminal participation in the wretched business," he said, " the men at the club are quite changed towards me."

" Idiots ! " I declared.

He sighed. " I'd give a lot to see J. M. H. now. . . ."

I felt a bit uncomfortable. *I* had been through no such ordeal as his, yet had been permitted to see J. M. H. ; and here was Toni, depressed, impoverished and in sore need of a Guru's advice. To tell him just now that both Lyall and I had visited J. M. H. seemed too cruel. This was obviously not the time to deliver the message. Toni looked at me in a strange manner, and I was reduced to silence.

Then he said slowly : " I believe you've seen J. M. H. . . ."

His assumption took me completely by surprise. Was I so poor an actor that my expression had given me away, or was Toni even more intuitive than I had thought ?

" Have you ? " he insisted after a pause.

" Yes," I admitted, but in my expression I tried to convey something of what I felt for him.

He said nothing ; far too loyal to our Guru to criticize him, or even to enter into a discussion with me as to why I had been favoured and he not. But I realized that he was both chagrined and puzzled.

I was wondering what I might say when Lyall Herbert came in. I had especially asked him to come along too, because it seemed to me now was the moment for Toni's true friends to rally round him. Lyall was full of sympathy, but although Toni was grateful, I could see he was preoccupied with his own thoughts. Presently he looked hard at Lyall, much as he had previously looked at me.

" I think you've seen J. M. H. too," he said at length.

Lyall was taken aback. He glanced at me, attempting to read my face.

" I've owned up," I said, " better do likewise."

" I thought as much," from Toni.

There was another constrained silence.

Should I deliver the message or not ? I tried to send a thought to J. M. H., hoping for an impression, but could get nothing.

Then suddenly my hand was forced : Toni asked point-blank : " Have you a message for me ? "

I admitted I had.

" And it is . . . ? "

" I'm afraid it's nothing very illuminating," I preluded.

" The message . . ." he urged.

" You're to go on in the old way—I mean with your meditation."

" Is that all ? "

" I'm sorry. . . ."

Toni looked disappointed and for some moments made no reply. " Have you a cigarette ? " he said at last with seeming irrelevance. I handed him one—surprised— for I had never known him smoke before. He puffed in silence for a while, then in his plaintive voice he mused : " Always the same thing, I have to get everything for myself and trust to my intuition, while you fellows . . ."

" But it's because *you* are further on than we are ! " Lyall interpolated, genuinely trying to console him. " After all, your intuition must be jolly good if you can sense at once whom we've been with."

" I've felt for some time that J. M. H. was in this country, but when I saw you, I knew it," Toni replied. After a pause he spoke again with an effort to be cheerful. " Ah, well, I suppose it's all part of one's training. . . . At any rate I'm glad my sensings were correct."

I couldn't help thinking what a plucky little fellow he was, outwardly so frail and sensitive, yet inwardly with the courage of a lion.

As he was about to leave that evening, he told us he had decided to go abroad for a while.

" It's the best thing I can do, in the circumstances," he said.

CHAPTER XV

MASTER KOOT HOOMI'S MESSENGER

" WE'VE got to find a cottage or something for the summer," Viola said, " and if we don't start looking round soon, we'll be left stranded. The doctor says somewhere high for me." She had just come down to breakfast and was turning over her pile of letters. " Hallo, here's a picture-postcard from David—at last —all scrawled round the steeple of the village church. . . . ' Am here,' " she read out, " ' marvellous Deva on hill-top. Cheery Taurus innkeeper with planets in earthy signs. Grub passable for this country. Progressed aspects improving. Love, David . . .' "

"Typical!" I laughed. "Why shouldn't we go down for a few days and sample the place ? We might hear of a cottage round there if we made inquiries."

The idea appealed to her. " But supposing he doesn't want us ? " she demurred.

" Send a prepaid wire and ask.   His lord-
ship can always make an excuse if he's
disinclined for our charming company. . . ."

But as it happened, he was not disinclined,
and wired that he would engage us rooms for
the week-end.

        *   *   *   *   *

The inn overlooked a vast expanse of
wooded country with downs in the distance,
and beyond them a vista of the sea.   Behind
the inn rose a bracken-covered hill, on the
summit of which a ring of tall pines encircled a
dew-pond like sentinels guarding a sacred pool.

We found David seated at a small iron table
in the picturesque garden laid out in terraces.

" Hallo, you egos ! " he greeted us cheerily,
" so you've arrived . . ."

He was looking all the better for his sojourn
in the country.

" The place seems to suit you," I remarked ;
and Viola added : " Yes, you're quite sun-
burnt ! "

" Plenty of Prana and Air-Devas about,
that's why," he answered, true to his usual
habit of handing out an occult explanation
for everything.

We laughed.   Though we could see no Air-

Devas ourselves, the place was certainly delightful, and the air bracing enough to warrant his allusion to " Prana."

We sat down at the little round table on which were writing-materials and a despatch-case. " What is it—horoscopes or letters ? " Viola inquired eagerly.

" Neither—book," was his terse reply.

" Ho-ho, at last ! " I exclaimed. " So that accounts for this sudden retreat into the country and adoption of the hermit's life. . . ."

" Just like you to act the dark horse and tell us nothing," Viola teased him. " What's the book about in particular ? One has to ask, because your repertoire's so large."

But he bundled his papers into the case, evidently in no mood for literary talk at the moment. " Tell you later, perhaps," he said. " I've been struggling with the wretched thing all morning—Saturn square Uranus and the day's bunch of bad lunars—nothing but frustrations; I'm fed-up with it. Let's go a walk."

" But I must have a bit of a rest first," my wife objected ; " if *you* had my wretched vehicle——"

" Sorry," he apologized, " I forgot."

" By the way, I've news," I told him;
" J. M. H. has turned up."

" I knew it, I knew it ! " he exclaimed
triumphantly, " didn't I sense the last time
we met that he'd turn up soon ! "

" You may have sensed it, but I may
remark that you didn't let on."

" I felt he didn't wish it."

" But you did see him—astrally ? "

" Who told you that ? "

" He told me himself."

David's smile was enigmatical. " Did he
say anything about me, apart from that ? "

" He said some very nice things—that your
' sensings ' are very reliable for one."

David's smile broadened with pleasure.

" What I want to know," Viola put in,
" is why he wouldn't see *me* ? He said *you*
could tell us."

David looked into space for a minute or
two. " You see, his vibrations are extremely
powerful, and while your health's so rotten,
they'd simply disorganize all your vehicles
and make you worse."

My wife was somewhat pacified.

" Hallo, Oooze—it's a lovely Oooze . . ."

This cryptic but affectionate-sounding remark was irrelevantly addressed by David to the inn cat, which had appeared on the scene, and was rubbing itself against his legs.

" *Our* poor cat has gone west, alas . . ." I said.   David had been very fond of it, and often used to pet it when he came to see us.

" I was afraid it must have," he replied sympathetically, " I saw its little astral vehicle the other night."

" Then it's not true that dogs and cats just return to the group-soul when they die ? " said Viola.

" Not if you've been really fond of them. Then you individualize them through love, and greatly hasten on their evolution.   Far more pets than you'd think get individualized. As a matter of fact, it was in the Master's garden that I've seen *your* cat since it's been dead."

" How delightful for the cat, and how charming of the Master ! " I exclaimed laughing, but nevertheless touched.

" It had a strong light round its head— showing it had been individualized—and looked lighter in colour than it did when alive," David went on.   " As for dogs, I once

MASTER KOOT HOOMI'S MESSENGER   183

saw a huge Airedale who'd been dead for
years go for a small Dark who was trying to
attack the mistress he'd been devoted to, and
give him ever such a biff."

" Well, I'm jolly glad to think the animals
we've loved still remain individuals ! " Viola
declared ; " I should hate to think of them
absorbed into something so vague as a group-
soul. . . .   And now if you like, I'm ready
for a walk."

The morning had been overcast, but now
a warm midday sun came through the clouds,
and the mingled fragrance of blossoms and
bracken and pine-trees filled the air. We
wandered for a while along woodland paths,
stopping now and then to rest on felled tree-
trunks and listen to the music of the rustling
leaves which formed a delicate and subtle
accompaniment to many a songful bird. It
was good to be in the country again, and my
mind wandered back to Sir Thomas and his
old-world garden. I would have liked to
describe it all to David, but of course could
not betray my trust.

After a while we strolled back to the inn.
The day was warm enough for lunch out of
doors, always a charming prospect, especially

in a country where the climate so seldom makes it possible.

During our meal, a crowd of young hikers, flushed and laughing, poured into the garden and settled themselves at a table a little way off.

" Don't you suffer rather from this kind of thing, especially at week-ends ? " Viola inquired of David ; " isn't it a bit disruptive to your work ? "

" They don't trouble me from that point of view," he returned, " and as a matter of fact——" He broke off, and for quite a while contemplated the noisy, chattering group in ruminative silence.

" As a matter of fact—what ? " Viola prompted him at last.

" Don't interrupt," I adjured her, " can't you see he's sensing them up ? "

" Correct," said David, " I was. I've been realizing for some time now that these hikers who pour out of the cities in search of beauty are one of the few hopeful signs of the age."

We glanced at him interrogatively, and he went on in an undertone :

" They're the sort of young egos who are being influenced by National Devas to get into closer touch with nature and its purer vibrations. They don't know it, of course, but that's neither here nor there. Some of the more refined are kind of led to definite centres, magnetized by Initiates centuries ago, and now guarded by Devas, some more, and some less powerful. Later, they will learn to visit these centres consciously."

" Yes, but what's their object—I mean, of the centres ? " I asked.

" Why, to train the advanced types of the race. You see, the psycho-spiritual atmosphere of magnetized spots is so strong that it acts as a great stimulus to the higher faculties. When these faculties have been sufficiently developed, then at any rate a portion of the race will be prepared for the coming of the Lord Maitreya at the end of the century."

" So I take it these hikers are a kind of prelude to great idealism," I suggested, " fore-runners, as it were, of a new type ? "

" Yes. You wait a few years and you'll see how it'll develop. Already there's a reaction from all that post-war gloom and licence, and we're beginning to see signs of much cleaner living and greater self-control.

Even now a league exists, formed by a group of young men, who've vowed to be faithful to their wives. . . . Wild oats are no longer fashionable amongst the upper classes, and instead we have early marriages, fidelity and offspring ! That's all an effort on the part of the Race-Devas to bring a higher type of soul into incarnation. Later on these Devas will be able to influence the race still more, because the response to their vibrations will become greater and greater. What with less promiscuity and one thing and another, a certain proportion of the race will become so sensitive that they'll actually be able to see the Devas and communicate with them. But of course that won't be just yet awhile, as you have at least to have etheric vision [1] for that.''

" I wish I could see the Devas," Viola said, as David paused to deal with his lunch ; " but even before I lost my bit of clairvoyance, I never actually saw them, though I could feel them."

" It's just a question of the type of clair-voyance or rather psychic faculty," David

---

[1] The type of clairvoyance by means of which nature-spirits, fairies and gnomes, etc., can be seen.

answered, " it varies so tremendously. Some egos can remember their past incarnations and see nothing at all ; others don't remember but can see auras and thought-forms ; others again only bring through memories of psychic experiences during sleep. Very few people possess the complete range of octaves through all the planes, as you might say. They'd have to be very highly trained clairvoyants indeed."

" Yet etheric vision is really the least subtle of all," I commented, " at least so I've been told."

" Yes, but even so it doesn't follow that you acquire that first," he rejoined; " it largely depends on your type of body and what sort of faculties you've acquired in past incars. All this business about the physical ether is very complex," he added. " I spent a lot of my time in India studying it, first under my Master and then on my own ; in fact, I've collected a lot of notes that are going into my book."

" Do let's hear ! " Viola said eagerly ; " nothing like trying it out on the dog. . . ."

He laughed and disappeared indoors to collect his manuscript. The hikers had departed, and quiet reigned once more in the garden, a fact for which we were grateful.

David returned with his precious despatch-case, and we retired to a little arbour lower down the garden where we would be free from interruptions.

" ' The ether,' " he read, " ' is the bridge between dense physical matter and the astral plane ; it has four sub-divisions, all inter-penetrating one another, and the fourth or densest ether is the one nearest to the physical plane. This fourth ether is the element in which those function who are animated by lusts, ambitions and desire for power in all forms. In the third ether, control over the aforementioned forces is gradually acquired by each individual for himself. In the second, the potential pupil in his physical body approaches the Path, and should become conscious of co-operating within an occult group towards bringing about the higher forms of group-discipline. If this is achieved suc-cessfully, the pupil may become a disciple of a Master, and given individual work to do. Such was the *old* order of development in the past, and was strictly maintained. Attempts to deviate from it by rushing into

the second ether before individual control
has been won and *adhered to*, often leads to
the creation of a terrible group-elemental
which is liable to poison the whole group
individually and can only be destroyed by
the dispersion of the group itself.' "

" Ah, now I understand why J. M. H. dis-
persed *his* group," I couldn't help interrupt-
ing. " Sorry. Go on."

" ' The positive qualities acquired by master-
ing the second ether may lead to conscious
co-operation with a Master or Masters on that
particular etheric line ; whilst by working in
the first ether, one becomes a full-fledged
occultist, functioning as a direct force on the
physical plane. All these subdivisions of the
ether are interpenetrated by astral, lower and
higher mental matter, and so forth, going
inwards in a fourth-dimensional manner. As
regards the vibrational rate of these sub-
divisions——' Oh, I've got to co-relate all
this properly," he broke off with surprising
abruptness, " before it can be given out."

" How tantalizing of you ! " Viola exclaimed. " Like the preliminary shots of next
week's film—' come again next Friday.' " . . .

*   *   *   *   *

It was a glorious Sunday morning, and the three of us climbed the hill and sat down by the dew-pond. From the plain below came the distant sound of church-bells, undulating on the breeze ; and overhead a sky-lark trilled its monotonous though joyous song.

" Our friend the Deva hovering over the hill, as usual," David remarked after a long silence.

" I thought so," from Viola. " I've seldom felt such a marvellous atmosphere."

" You often find these National Devas in places overlooking a wide expanse like this," David pursued. " I've seen and heard them communicating with each other by lovely sort of flashings of colour and sound. . . . But it's hopeless to describe it in words. . . . How trying," he exclaimed unexpectedly after a pause, " other egos biffing in to spoil everything ! "

A picnic party had appeared on the brow of the hill, talking and laughing with considerable vulgarity.

" Is our Deva aware of them at all, do you suppose ? " my wife asked as they drew nearer.

" Not of this lot, I should think ; they're far too crude and low-geared ! "

" Well, what price us ? " I jested.

" He'd be aware of people like you right enough, because he realizes you love beauty. I've frequently noticed that Devas do respond to egos with real artistic feeling. Their auras seem to expand and glow as if they were pleased with the appreciation lavished upon their surroundings."

" By the way," I inquired, as the voices of the noisy party, much to our relief, receded in the distance, " do Devas ever take pupils, like Masters do ? "

" Not Devas of this kind, because they're restricted to the centres they guard." He went on to tell us, however, that certain advanced types of Air-Devas sometimes over-shadow, and so inspire, musicians and poets. They even make personal links with them and prepare them for the taking of certain Deva initiations. These latter are neverthe-less quite different from human initiations, and can only be regarded as initiatory rites for candidates who aspire to transfer to the Deva line of evolution in some future life. " For instance, both Wagner and Swinburne were overshadowed by Devas," he informed us, " and Wagner's Deva still helps to maintain the Wagner tradition, by detailing off his subordinates to inspire those who perform that great composer's music. Needless to say, Devas of this kind are not restricted to any one country. . . ." David lit a cigarette and puffed in silence for a while, dreamily watching the blue smoke dissolve in the air.

" I suppose you'd call those *International* Devas as opposed to National ones," I observed.

" Certainly. Their job is to link up different countries, not only through music, art and literature, but as far as possible through politics as well. It's these great International Devas who are trying, in conjunction with the Masters, to bring about Co-operation. Just as Sound-Devas may be seen clairvoyantly presiding, as it were, at an important concert, so International Devas preside at important political conferences. First of all, they work to bring them about, and then they overshadow them to try and preserve harmony and achieve the desired result. It may interest you egos to know that the Devas and the Masters are co-operating to combine the best characteristics of the Americans and the British to form the nucleus

of the future race. The Americans are more
intuitive and open to the higher planes than
other races, but they haven't the stability of
the British. Blend the two, and a gentler
and finer type will be the result—a type which,
step by step, will be able to conquer the sub-
divisions of the physical ether,[1] and learn to
work consciously with the Masters and the
Devas in centuries to come."

" In short," I summed up, " the Devas are
highly important entities, and the sooner the
generality of mankind knows something about
them, the better, eh ? "

He nodded.   " There's going to be a good
deal along that line in my book."

More people were arriving on the hill-side.

" Ow, look, Mar—wot a luvly view . . .
wot's that plice hover there ? "

" Wait till I git me breath, dear, I'm fair
pumped, I am. . . ." This from a stout
female toiling up the path behind her offspring.

It was a little too much for our susceptibilities.

" I think a walk now," Viola said to David ;
" we want to cast our eye over possible
domiciles for the summer."

[1] See *ante*.

" Come along," he exclaimed, jumping to his feet, " there's a charming cottage with a board up about half a mile from the village. . . ."

*   *   *   *   *

Sunday evening. . . .

The holiday-makers had all left for their homes. A roseate sun was sinking to rest behind the far-off downs. All was still. We had found a seat on the edge of a wood, from which we could see the vast plain beneath us, violet-tinted in the vesperal haze. The fresh leaves exhaled a sweet fragrance, and the smoke from a newly lit log-fire, issuing from a cottage near by, suggested the smell of incense.

David was in one of his silent moods, lost in meditation. But at length he said : " One of Master K. H.'s Music-Devas is here . . . I think it's the one who overshadowed your friend Chris during her lifetime. . . ."

There was another pause, in which I could see that David was listening tensely. Then he said : " It conveys a picture to me in colour and sound—but how to get it over to you. . . ? "

" Do try," Viola implored him.

He did not answer immediately ; and when at last he spoke his voice sounded as if he were listening to something very far off :

" Master K. H. hears night and day the cry of anguish rising up from the hearts of suffering humanity. . . . Like a great crescendo, it swells and swells. . . . How shall He answer it ? . . . He will send a willing Messenger, one whose work shall not be accomplished through speech, but through Sound . . . Sound to heal the wounds dealt by the clash and conflict of words . . . Sound to bring back Love and Joy and Tranquillity to a darkened world . . . Sound which subtly and secretly will mingle with those Devic forces striving to bring about Peace between Nation and Nation . . . And by the greatness of the world's need shall be measured the greatness of that Messenger's power. . . ."

" Chris . . . ! " we both cried simultaneously, almost in spite of ourselves.

But David would say no more ; he merely smiled, and continued to gaze into space.

CHAPTER XVI

TWO HIMALAYAN MASTERS

A LONG rainy summer which was no summer had passed : yet not uneventfully, for we had taken the cottage David had discovered, and within its quiet walls had learnt many a strange and interesting thing, as our friend collected a variety of occult data for his book.

September brought beautiful warm sunny days, but with regret we had returned to London, bringing David with us.

Not a word from J. M. H., and I had just begun to wonder whether the " time not specified " would draw out into years, when a letter came with directions for Herbert and myself to visit him the following week.

The blue car met us at the station ; and as we drove along, we could not help speculating as to what might be in store for us.

We had just passed the lodge gates, when

to our astonishment we saw Toni Bland.   We
drew up, and he got into the car.

"Good   heavens!"   we   exclaimed,   "*you*
. . ."

He smiled.   "I suppose you thought I'd
evaporated for ever."

"Well, considering I rang you up and was
told that nobody knew where you were . . ."

"You're looking extremely well—full of
beans," Herbert remarked.   "Very different
from the last time we saw you."

"Ah, much has happened since then," Toni
replied.   But by then we had drawn up at
the front door.

"Mr. Haig's at the lily-pond," the old-
school butler informed us as he took our
suit-cases.   "He requested me to ask you
to join him there when you arrived.   Should
you not know the way, doubtless Mr. Bland
will conduct you. . . ."

"Come along," said Toni, twinkling.

J. M. H. had lost that slightly fatigued look
I had noticed the last time we met.

"Greetings, my friends," he said, advancing
to meet us and giving us each a hand.   "You
were surprised to see Toni, eh?"   He put a
hand on the latter's shoulder and looked at

him benignly. " Well, well, there are even more surprises awaiting you. . . ."

Toni withdrew, and we seated ourselves beside J. M. H. on the curved stone seat overlooking the pond.

" What news do you bring me ? " he asked ; and immediately Mrs. Saxton came to my mind. I told him she had passed over ; but felt I was only telling him what he knew already.

" I sent you a mental S.O.S. just before she went," I said ; " did you get it ? "

He shook his head. " I was in deep meditation at the time."

" Yet I feel sure a Master *did* come to her ! "

" All Masters are one in spirit, and a selfless thought directed towards the White Lodge will never go unanswered. It was Master K. H. who responded to your call. He has since told me so."

Then I realized with gratitude that my surmise had been correct. But aloud I said : " Is she happy ? "

" As happy as one may be who has but little love in her heart, yet far happier than if she had passed over unguided and uncared-for, and in the state of doubt into which she had previously been plunged."

He turned to Herbert. " You have written those articles I suggested ? "

" Yes, I have."

" We have decided that after all the book would be more useful ; and I intend to give you some further details for it while you are here."

Lyall's expression showed the elation he felt.

Suddenly I remembered a letter that was in my pocket.

" Talking of books," I said to J. M. H., " here's a letter that concerns you. The writer is certainly not puffed up with his own importance. It arrived this morning—may I show it you or not ? "

He smiled and held out his hand.

" Having perused books by your voluble self *re* Initiate," J. M. H. read aloud, " am much dumbfounded, gratified and uplifted to be informed that inestimable Yogis do not exist only in country of my mother's womb, but that pearls of our wisdom have pierced into Europe and U.S.A. Did personally aspire to sit at feet of incomparable Yogi in M—— but found myself tearfully lacking in necessary sanctimonious qualifications, so feared to receive metaphysical foot-kick from said Yogi, if had presented self as chela. Books of yours for which paid rupees four, have given many lakhs worth of condolence to soul subterraneously immersed. Offer sea of gratitude to Mahatma J. M. H. for assurance transmitted kindly via your unassuming self, that surcease of intermittent marital consummations (see chaps. on Theosophists and Marriage) is not first prerequisite to life spiritual. Vice versa is asseverated by local ascetics. Am passionate but painstaking Babu.

P.S. Aspire to become chela of said Mahatma in subsequent incarnation. . . ."

He handed it back with an amused smile, remarking as he did so : " You will not be able to answer that letter."

" Oh—why ? "

" Haven't you observed there's no address on it ? "

Strangely enough, I had not. " I suppose he must have forgotten," I said.

" You are mistaken ; he's so genuinely modest that he doesn't even expect an answer. You remember the parable of the Publican and the Pharisee ? "

" *God be merciful to me a sinner . . .*" I quoted.

" This man is a true example of the lesson that was intended to convey. . . . And now," he pursued, " there is something of importance I must tell you both. I am going into seclusion for some time. I am going on the Continent, to a little place high up among mountains, where I shall spend most of my time in deep meditation. I shall have one chela with me to guard my body while it is in trance, but only one, because my work among groups is over. Whether it will be resumed later depends on many things. Although there is a general plan for Mankind laid down by the Great Ones, remember that no one is an automaton, and not even the Masters or the Devas can foreknow how the denizens of earth will react to the details of that Plan. The great road may be hewn through the mountains, but the wayfarers may linger on the way, or be deterred from pursuing their journey by innumerable happenings unforeseen by any save the Lords of Karma. To co-operate with the Masters in dealing with the problems that will beset the remaining years of this Dark Cycle, is to be my dharma.[1] To this end a change in my own development is necessary, for I have to learn to contact the higher cosmic ethers, and study their relationship to the earth as it is at the present time. This can only be accomplished in complete retirement and in a state of long-protracted Samadhi." [2]

There was silence. I felt sad, and I knew that Lyall was feeling sad also. " Then we are to lose our Guru," I said at last.

He smiled lovingly. " Not lose," he said; " have you forgotten that the link between chela and Guru is the strongest of all links ? "

" But even our thoughts don't seem to reach you when you're in such profound meditation . . ." I was thinking of my S.O.S. in connection with Mrs. Saxton.

" Yes, and what about all the people who have grown to love you through his books ? " queried Lyall with a glance at me.

" Did I not say that every thought directed to a Brother of the White Lodge is bound to obtain a response ? " His voice was very gentle. " Let me tell you something that perhaps neither of you know. There are those on the

---

[1] A combination of duty and mission.
[2] Super-conscious trance.

Path who have imagined themselves to be pupils of one Master, when all the time they have been pupils of another. They have even been transferred from one Master to another without realizing it in their waking consciousness. Our friend here has been allowed to write his books, not to advertise me in particular—though I'm afraid that has rather been the result—but to apprise his public of the existence of the Masters in general : and this not for the Masters' benefit, but for that of their pupils and potential pupils. Never forget that all the Masters are One. . . . They are the great Servants of Humanity. But it is not for the pupil to select some Master because he has a particular leaning towards Him—but for the Master to select the pupil because of certain qualifications the latter may possess, which may be trained along His particular line and so prove useful in serving Mankind."

There was another silence, during which the two of us pondered upon what we had just been told. At last Lyall said, so ingenuously that J. M. H. had to laugh : " I must say, it seems a bit strange to think of anyone meditating the *whole* day. . . ! "

"You don't realize that meditation of that sort is great bliss—the bliss of physical rest combined with intense super-physical activity."

"Then I suppose we must be glad," murmured Lyall.

"Yes—then I suppose we must be glad . . ." I echoed.

He pressed our hands by way of answer. "Wait," he said. "Do you think I asked you here merely to give you the sadness of saying good-bye. . . ?"

*   *   *   *   *

Sir Thomas, J. M. H., Lyall and I were together in the library after dinner.

"The Masters are in a quandary," said the old gentleman, addressing me. "What use Teachers with no one to teach? What use Servants with no one to serve? *You* can be of assistance."

I was more than astonished, and wondered in what possible way I could help.

"A third book," he continued in his terse manner. "Have we not supplied you with material? Your astrological friend has also supplied you with material. You have made observations yourself. Write them down."

" But am I competent to do it with any measure of success ? "

" Tut, tut, *we* shall see to that. . . ." He turned to Lyall. " And you," he said, " you will write a new kind of music—as well as a book on the subject—for which you will receive special preparatory training at a Master's hands. Etheric vision necessary to compose this new music. Essential that the values of certain combinations of notes, and their effect on the listeners, be fully realized by composers before it be given forth."

Lyall's face lit up.

" Music a very important force in evolution," Sir Thomas went on. " Bad music— bad morals. Old music—old ideas and lack of progress. Church music of to-day, for instance, what is it ? " He shook his head. " Hymns that are an insult to musical intelligence, yet supposed to be pleasing to the Deity. Gregorian chants—well, well, pleasant and quaint ; but no effect on auras of present generation. Never intended for twentieth century. Something different required." He smiled benevolently and turned to leave us. " Come to the Blue Room at ten o'clock to-morrow," he added as he went out.

" Do you think Sir Thomas wants me to specialize in church music in future ? " Lyall asked somewhat cautiously.

J. M. H. laughed. " No, no. I daresay you may write a little church music among other things, but Sir Thomas merely alluded to it because it's so particularly behind the times." He proceeded to explain that recently an attempt had been made by the Masters to stimulate an interest in occult ceremonial by the introduction of what was erroneously thought to be suitable music, but the average thinking persons in the outside world of to-day proved too sophisticated to benefit much by it, while those within the movement were too involved in their own inhibitions and personal problems. The magnetism became tainted by personality-worship, and the music which should have enhanced the ritual was too old-fashioned to produce the desired effect. Thus the organization from which much had been hoped—because so free from intolerance, bigotry and sectarianism—proved a disappointment in the end. The *Intelligentsia* who might have joined it were deterred from doing so, while the rank and file obtain all they require from the already existing religious communities.

" This more liberal organization," he went on, " was originally intended to combat the wave of scepticism which some of the Masters foresaw would attack the more cultured classes. The devotional types feel the need of a religion : but if they happen to be intellectual as well as devotional, the ordinary exoteric forms of Christianity fail to satisfy them. The result is that thousands of people with neither the time nor the inclination to study comparative Religion, Mysticism or Occultism, are left in a condition of Doubt —doubt in the existence of the Higher Powers, doubt in an after-life, and so forth. This must not of course be regarded as a sin, but it does tend to atrophy the higher mental body and the spiritual faculties, and as you know already, may lead to a prolonged state of unconsciousness on the other planes after death. In other words, doubt builds a wall round the subtler bodies, and interferes with their freedom. If you bind a limb and restrict its freedom for too long, it atrophies. Very well, then. The new church having met with inadequate response, we must now call art,

and especially music, to our aid. What ceremonial can no longer accomplish, a new form
of music *may* and we trust *will* ; and it will
be your mission and that of later composers
to bring this music down on to the physical
plane."

" A new type of music to come through ! "
Lyall exclaimed joyously ; " that's good news
indeed. The fear of becoming antiquated
always pursues me. What boredom have I
not suffered from being forced to listen to the
works of antiquated composers."

We laughed. . . .

Herbert and I were to return to town the
following day, and I particularly dreaded
saying good-bye to J. M. H. Since my early
childhood I have found leave-taking a trying
ordeal, and somehow the years have not
tended to diminish its pathos for me.

Perhaps it was because J. M. H. realized
this, that on bidding me good-night that
evening, he said : " Because to-morrow is a
day of parting, do not think that you will
never see me again." . . . He laid his hand
on my arm for a moment, smiled and was
gone.

He did not appear for breakfast the next morning, and I wondered why; but Toni Bland told me afterwards that he had breakfasted long ago in his room.

'" Are you travelling back to town with us, by any chance ? " I asked Toni.

" No," he replied.

" Lucky man. . . . But we shall see you soon, I hope ? "

He shook his head. " I'm going abroad again and shall not come back for a long time. You've been a good friend to me," he said as we started to wander down the garden path, " and I'm sorry to leave you, but——"

He never completed the sentence, for just then Sir Thomas came round the bend of the path with his dog in attendance.

" Come," he said, looking at his watch and addressing me, " it is close on ten o'clock."

Suddenly Toni grasped my hand, pressed it, but said nothing. I wondered why, as I hurried after Sir Thomas. Did it mean I was about to go through some test and he wished me well—or what ? I had not forgotten that Sir Thomas had requested us to come to the

Blue Room at ten o'clock, but my watch was a bit slow.

We found J. M. H. and Lyall in the long gallery waiting for us. Sir Thomas nodded to them, smiled, proceeded to unlock the door of that mysterious apartment, and bade us enter. There were four chairs in a semicircle facing the beautiful stained-glass window from which gold and purple rays slanted down and illuminated our faces. Sir Thomas and J. M. H. took the two middle chairs, and we sat on the outer ones.

There was a long silence. Then Sir Thomas touched the centre of my forehead for a few moments with his fingers. " Listen . . ." he said.

From far away I heard the strains of an organ with which was mingled the sound of voices so pure and ethereal as to suggest the chanting of a celestial choir, wafted on a peaceful evening breeze. The music was unlike any music I had heard before ; it was subtle, yet melodious, sweet, yet devoid of all sentimental lusciousness ; at one moment powerful and awe-awakening, at another soft and tender as the caress of an angel's hand.

" My Brother Koot Hoomi playing on His

organ . . . and the voices you hear are those of the Gandharvas. . . . Listen well, and remember, for one day you shall give forth such music to the world. . . ."

It was Sir Thomas who had spoken, and his words were addressed to Lyall.

The music continued for a while, then gradually faded away, and there was another silence.

" Close your eyes," he said, " and see with your inner vision."

Suddenly I became sensible of a sweet fragrance as of mingled flowers ; and then, although my eyes were closed, the forms of two Beings appeared through a haze of the purest and most lovely shades of colour I have ever seen. And at that moment I realized I was beholding Master Koot Hoomi—Who had spoken to me through Chris—and with Him was the Tibetan Adept, Master D. K.

" Greetings, my Brothers," Sir Thomas said quietly, and Master Koot Hoomi's Christ-like face was illumined by a smile so tender and ineffable that it seemed the very essence of those words He had spoken to Chris long ago : " *The love that I feel for each one of you, that is God. . . .*"

The Tibetan Master smiled also, and a paternal sweetness suffused his Mongolian features and awoke in me an intense feeling of devotion.

J. M. H.'s voice very gently broke the silence.

" Brothers and Masters," he said, " into your keeping I give my beloved chelas who have served me well.   May they prove worthy of your guidance, your protection and your love."

Master Koot Hoomi stretched out His arms to us in loving welcome, and in His eyes was a look of recognition, as if to say : " Have we not spoken with each other before ? " Then His lips moved and I seemed to hear Him say : " Long years ago in Greece when I was Pythagoras, you were both my pupils, and now I welcome you back to me again. You who desire to serve humanity shall be given greater power to serve—you, with your pen, and you "—he turned to Lyall—" with your music.   We would bring back to a suffering and perplexed world some of the ancient ways of healing the sick ; and one of these is healing by musical sound.   Man shall be taught that he who would heal the gross physical body which he can see must first heal the *linga sharira*,[1] which as yet he cannot see. To this end we need those who would serve us with their divers gifts, that serving us they may serve Mankind. Very great is our need in this age of darkness and doubt, for those who once were willing to serve, serve us no more, and those who might have been willing to serve, and so reap the joys of service, have turned away and are lost to us in the gloom."

And then the vision began to fade. I felt that the two Masters were still there, but I was losing the power to see. With an involuntary movement I put out my hand towards Sir Thomas, that he might touch my forehead again and enable me to perceive once more ; but he signified that it would not be well to do so.

Then J. M. H. spoke, first addressing Lyall and then myself. " Master Koot Hoomi says that His Brother, Master D. K., will prepare your subtler bodies to receive the inspiration which ultimately He will give you Himself ; and that several of the Masters will help you to write the book about which Sir Thomas, at Their request, has spoken to you."

[1] Etheric double.

He paused for a moment. " Although I may go away into seclusion, none of those who have honoured me with their love and have become linked to me by their thoughts shall be left without a guide. Master Koot Hoomi extends His hands and says : ' Let them come to us ; according to their needs and according to their aspiration to serve us, so shall it be given them. . . .' He bestows on you both His blessing."

We sat for a few minutes in silence, then Sir Thomas and J. M. H. rose from their seats.

" Remain here quietly for a while," Sir Thomas said, " and then go to the lily-pond."

And indeed we were glad of the injunction, for in that room there lingered such an atmosphere of peacefulness and love that I was loath to leave it, even for the sweet tranquillity of Sir Thomas's garden. Moreover, my whole consciousness was suffused with a spiritual exhilaration so new and wonderful that I almost feared to move lest it should depart from me and be lost, never to be regained.

We had been contemplating the lily-pond in silence for a while when, much to our surprise, Sir Thomas approached, and sat down beside us.

" Farewells——" he said, " few of us like them, and most of us could dispense with them ; so why not avoid them ? Yet to him who is unified with all beings, and realizes the One Self, there is no parting. Ah—well. . . . That realization will be yours one day. Meanwhile—tut, tut, the old gentleman is left to do all the talking and break the news. . . ."

J. M. H. had saved us the ordeal of a good-bye, and had gone, taking Toni Bland with him as the one chela.

THE END